DEATH
AT OLANA

GLENDA RUBY

DEATH
AT OLANA

GLENDA RUBY

This is entirely a work of fiction.
While Frederic Church's home, Olana, obviously does exist,
all names, characters, businesses, organizations, places, events,
and incidents are the product of the author's imagination
and are used fictitiously.
Any resemblance to actual persons, living or dead, events,
or locales is entirely coincidental.

Library of Congress Cataloguing-in-Publication data is on file
with the Library of Congress

ISBN 978-0-615831145

MANUFACTURED IN
THE UNITED STATES OF AMERICA

GREENDALE BOOKS

FIRST EDITION

For Ros

DEATH
AT OLANA

GLENDA RUBY

PRELUDE TO A PARTY

Thursday last. My thoughts: Aren't you vaguely apprehensive about dressing for a party you do not wish to attend?

Distractions become priorities. Do I want a dressing drink? What to have? A glass of wine? Tiny little martini? Tiny little Manhattan? Must have a thimble of something to encourage me as I face the closet.

Naturally, not caring to go, I have given no thought to what to wear. Ah! The old black Valentino. Worn to every party since Satan was in short pants. I haul that out again. Thank God, still no moths. Black silk slacks. Quickly polish ancient black heels the Smithsonian keeps calling about.

Get into the mood, dear, if you are going to go. Play some music. Chet Baker? Too morose. Xavier Cugat? Too frisky. Louis Prima? Might not make it at all. Paul Desmond? Exactly.

Clothes and makeup hurled into their places, I step from the living room onto the porch to polish off thimble and preview the night. It is cold but magnificent. Black mountains loom enormous. The moon makes a wake on the river. A tugboat, brightly lit, chugs toward Albany past the channel marker blinking green. The hemlocks around the yard are dark silhouettes, as are odds and ends of porch furniture that never made it to the cellar after Indian summer. I sigh, come in, put thimble in sink, don coat, head down path to car.

Frigid. With the wind chill factor, which from childhood I have thought to be the "windshield" factor, it must be 10°.

That night, I preferred to remain at home. My rack of lamb was marinating in its lemon and rosemary. I'd have had another thimble. Read by the fire.

All things considered, there was no good reason to leave the house last Thursday.

Would I have felt differently had I known I was going to a murder?

1

You may be wondering who I am.

I'm a garden variety Northeast transplant from the South who went to school in Washington hell bent on public service---but wound up working as a spook. Or an operative. Or an enabler. I was never sure which. Never got a position description.

Majored in English, history, and art history; visited Winterthur and became fascinated with furniture and the decorative arts. Got a master's. Moved to New York as a baby curator at an auction house. Went to London to view a collection and was lunching alone one day in the Connaught Bar when an attractive American man seated at an adjacent table began to chat.

He joined me for coffee after lunch, then invited me to dinner to discuss a "business matter." Over filet and Petrus, he asked if I was aware that antiques and other pretty old things could lead one down unusual trails. What sort of trails, I asked. He said trails to money. Happy day, said I. He explained that traffic in antiquities was not only big business, but also that money and other things sometimes traveled concealed in antiques. Like what, I said? This and that, he suggested. And he asked if I would help him out on one thing. So I did. And then another.

Gradually I began to know some of the more important "collectors" who, indeed, were collecting considerably more than Louis XV or armorial faience.

In reasonably short order, I became an expert on secret drawers, removable panels, and other interesting things that can be done with furniture, art, and crates when one wants to move small things from one place to another without being detected.

And small items can be so many different, interesting, *valuable* things. They can be art, securities, unfortunate letters or other damning correspondence. They can be coded messages. By the time I was at the end of my career they had even become little hunks of DNA.

You may recall the theft of a small Klimt from a private collection in The Hague? It appeared in the back of a Bauhaus commode I retrieved at auction.

A certain map was taken from the Vatican museum. Popes are notoriously tight-lipped about this sort of thing. On their eminent behalf we discreetly asked a few questions. The whole thing is knowing who deals in what----and we know. We surmised the map was going to a private collector in Grosse Pointe who purported to have an interest solely in a pair of game tables being deaccessioned by an estate in Amsterdam. The gaming tables had invisible drawers for hiding aces---or a map, as it turned out.

The key to a Swiss safe deposit box wandered away from its owner and was recovered in a hidden compartment within one arm of a Trafalgar chair being shipped to his ex-wife. Another happy ending, but not for the ex-wife, as you may imagine.

As funding flowed from my secret friends, I opened an auction house, followed in a few years by European branches.

My career was considerably more lucrative than public service but no less taxing and so I have chosen to take early retirement in this charming area, the Hudson Valley.

But, alas, from time to time, circumstances arise which dictate that I assume the old mantle of, well, law enforcement, I suppose. Detective work. I don't tell anyone up here about my background. Let's keep it our little secret.

Here I am known for my expertise in 18th and 19th Century furniture and the decorative arts. My ability to comment at some length on marquetry or the lineage of a particular finial has stood me in good stead in the country of upstate New York. I consult, I decorate, I dabble in real estate.

Now, in the shank of youth, I am still reasonably attractive, although I somehow never married, alas, and so have had to forego naming twin girls Ormulu and Trellis.

◆◆◆◆◆

Most of the charming people and the ne'er-do-wells, the heroes and the villains who populate this tale, abide in Columbia County, about two hours north of New York.

While this area is still very much the country, predominantly agricultural and rural, about twenty-five years ago there began a diaspora of New York City cognoscenti who chose to spend their weekends in quaint---though, to be frank, they do have their homely aspects---hamlets and villages, rather than amid haute bourgeois excess on, say, Long Island, to choose a random example.

And so among the apple, pear, peach, and cherry orchards, the dairy farms, and the good local people who run them, you will increasingly find upper middle, indeed, wealthy families, singles, straights and gays, painters, writers, publishers, lawyers, and media types who have migrated to this historic area. We all believe we live in the most beautiful place in the world, mostly on weekends.

The Valley's current complement of weekenders, a pejorative term among the locals, was preceded by legions of Astors, Vanderbilts, Delanos, Roosevelts, and Rockefellers, these last who hail from these parts, who made their weekend and summer homes along the banks of the Hudson River, drawn by the scenic grandeur and the privacy. These early white tribes were acclaimed for their vast fortunes and public service--- signing the Declaration of Independence, building railroads, endowing libraries, monopolizing steel, or governing us.

Here they were also acclaimed for building splendid mansions, idiosyncratic castles and villas with walnut or locust allees, for maintaining vast staffs and well-manicured croquet pitches.

5

As you know, the Hudson River School of painting began here. One of the jewels in the area's crown is the Moorish Persian fantasy, Olana, a residence created by the famed landscape artist, Frederic Church.

Olana reigns from a six hundred foot hill overlooking the Hudson River and its valley. When I arrived in the first wave of the Manhattan diaspora twenty-five years ago, the last surviving Church heir had recently died. Our good governor, himself a Rockefeller and no stranger to munificent public works, and well-goaded by his in-law Elizabeth, who invented historic preservation hereabouts, stepped in to rescue Olana from the auctioneer's gavel.

The marvelous old house subsequently became a ward of the State, with a modest annual budget for upkeep---a 501c3. This sleepy not-for-profit was propped up by a meager band of local and weekend enthusiasts giving unremarkable sums for support. A complement of sweet local ladies versed in the history of the artist and his home shepherded sporadic visitors through the house. In the early days, I invariably booked my guests for tours of Olana; their favorite game was 'Stump the Docent'.

Back then, Olana's annual members' meetings were nondescript assemblages of perhaps forty or so earnest types in chinos or dowdy dirndls. Occasionally some dowager would appear in a picture window hat. Fund-raisers consisted mostly of paying ten dollars to enjoy a picnic you'd packed yourself. In those days, halcyon, I now see in retrospect, the annual members' Christmas party found piles of Raindeers and Agway rubber boots piled at the front door so as not to track in snow. The punch featured an *île flotant* of orange sherbet. The sparkling wine was from the coast of Spain.

All that has now changed. Olana has become chic. Its fundraisers entail writing checks in four, five, even six digits; its donors' parties are held in glittering New York triplexes and galleries as well as *in situ*.

And so it was with a touch of nostalgia for simpler times past that I dressed for this year's Christmas party on a cold, snowy evening, hauling out the old black Valentino tunic yet again and slipping into a pair of black duppioni slacks. Out the door I went, escorted by my faithful butler, Bennett.

Even though Olana's mile of winding, steadily climbing driveway had been plowed several times and sanded, there are enough hairpin turns to make the ascent a little tricky in snow and ice. After negotiating our way to the top of the hill, Bennett and I were more than ready for a drink. We entered to find the old house looking especially grand, its Victorian excesses charming in candlelight. Every mantle, every doorway was swagged with evergreens, every chandelier bristled with mistletoe, and on the landing a quartet in medieval garb held forth with *The Holly and the Ivy*.

More than two hundred people in black tie or seasonal finery stood throughout the downstairs rooms, sipping Roederer and enjoying the hors d'oeuvres circulated by extremely toothsome young waiters.

The big excitement tonight---and the only reason we had been pried away from my hearth-- -was to be the presentation of a new Church painting, acquired from an anonymous donor. A wine-red moiré drapery billowed beside the musicians on the landing, concealing the painting until its unveiling. Wading into the throng, I heard snatches of conversation about the stock market, television deals, saw business cards being exchanged. I really must get some cards at some point. There was not a dirndl in sight but the Italian designers were well represented.

A photographer circulated, snapping candids.

I heard my name being called. Turning, I found myself in the arms of Maureen Lodge, the arts reporter for the *Times*, and an old friend from New York City.

"Maureen! Merry Christmas! We've clearly hit the big time if you're covering this party!"

"My darling girl! Joyeaux Noel for daaaaaays. Kiss, kiss. You look too divine."

"That's sweet of you to say, Maureen, and fortunate since I often wear this."

"Marvelous crowd tonight for the unveiling, what? Oh, here's your adorable butler!" Bennett presented two glasses to us, then snagged one for himself from a passing tray.

We were joined by Eve Healy, a tall, rangy blonde. As Olana's behind-the-scenes administrator, Eve makes the place function.

"Greetings, all! Great to see you!" Eve said.

"Eve, everything looks beautiful! Say hello to Maureen Lodge. She's covering the party for the *Times*. Maureen, this is Eve Healy. She works here and knows everything. You should interview her and her boss, Sheila. By the by, where is Sheila?"

"Oh, she's around," Eve said, beckoning to a waiter. "Here, try the canapés. They're by a new group from across the river called 'Who Did This?'"

Maureen said, "I must say, the waiters are deck these halls dishy tonight. But of course really all anyone can talk about is the new painting."

Bennett asked, "Has anybody figured out where it came from? And who's the mystery donor?"

Maureen replied, "He's over there. Beard, blue jacket. Thus far I haven't pried anything out of him, but I will. This is the biggest art story since the Gardner heist."

Olana has several marvelous, small Church sunsets and studies of the local mountains done in his later years but, as you probably know, he was a big time *plein aire* guy. His most famous paintings, reflecting his world travels, are enormous----say, 35 feet by 25---and couldn't possibly fit into the house. Church made his fortune by touring those canvasses throughout the United States. Thousands upon thousands of simple citizens paid $.25, the equivalent of $25 today, to gaze in wonder at a Peruvian landscape, a Mexican volcano, or a forbidding clutch of icebergs. Since his every work had been catalogued and researched, as far as anyone knew, curiosity about the provenance of a 'new' Church painting was more than justified.

Maureen offered her opinion on the painting's provenance. "Lots of money says it's from when Church was in the Middle East, been in a private collection, has never been seen before. Aren't there are rumors of a Church dalliance in South America? Are Church's diaries here? I should review them. This is the biggest art story since the Sistine Chapel."

Leaving Maureen to have Eve introduce her to quotable notables for her article, Bennett and I moved into the dining room to admire the decorative excesses of a Victorian Yuletide recreated for our nostalgic appreciation. Therein we happened upon Helen Spriggins, Olana's head docent, who was lecturing several guests who gazed at several Old Masters hung above the sideboard.

A stout and imperious matron, Helen was in her element, holding the floor and gesturing dramatically with a pointer toward the paintings.

" Not only did Mr. Church acquire a collection of old masters," she gravely intoned, "but he then *retouched* them! These whiskers for example...NOT in the original! This cherub? NOT in the original!"

"Good evening, Helen," I ventured when she had concluded her remarks. Helen has yet to succumb to my sparkling personality.

"Oh, Miss Brooks," Helen replied. "Taking a break from your hectic designing schedule? And you are....?" She raised her eyebrows and contemplated Bennett, handsome in his tuxedo.

"Good evening, Madame. Bennett Holbrook."

Helen pressed on. "And you are....?"

"Bennett lives in my guest cottage, Helen. He's a painter."

Bennett smiled. "I'm pleased to say I am actually Ms. Brooks' butler, Mrs. Spriggins."

Mrs. Spriggins' eyebrows moved a full inch north.

"Really!?? Her *butler*......."

I countered this with, "You've outdone yourself, Helen! The decorations are superb!"

Bennett asked, "Where did you find those enormous ferns?"

Mrs. Spriggins simpered, "Don't you adore them! They're so *pleistocene*. This year, our ostrich ferns were flown in from Jamaica, and genuine Japanese peacock plumes from Kyoto!"

"And these gorgeous orchids?"

"Imported from 28th Street," Helen informed us. "Have you seen William?" she asked.

"Not yet. Why?"

"When you do, you might ask him to keep his temper under control, now that we have guests," advised Mrs. Spriggins. She swept from the room.

I turned to Bennett. "Why did you tell her you're my butler? That'll drive her crazy."

"Because I *am* your butler, dear. Do let's make an effort to remember that."

As Bennett and I strolled back into the center hall, I saw my old pal Martha Lee waltzing through the crowd, Champagne in hand. Martha is slightly zaftig but has a very pretty face. She wore a red cape over purple velvet tights and a green velvet fascinator in her lovely dark hair

"Martha!" I cried.

"Hey, Kiddo! Merry Christmas! How's my favorite ex-spy Sister Parrish wannabe? And the pseudo butler." She kissed Bennett warmly, then sang out, "Uh-oh! Here comes trouble!"

We all turned to see our neighbor, Huxley Smythe, approaching. Dapper in a green velvet smoking jacket, dark evening trousers, and a formal shirt with the tie untied, Hux is an elegantly impressive presence, tall, and eightyish. His aristocratic hauteur leavened by wry wit, Huxley's frequent conversational gambit is to be an *agent provocateur*.

"Tie this damn thing!" Hux snapped as Martha and I planted simultaneous kisses on his cheeks. "Good evening, ladies, Bennett."

I moved to the task but was jostled aside by Martha .

"Let me. Here, Lindsey, hold this." She thrust her glass into my hand and assaulted Huxley's tie. "Come closer, Hux!"

Mouth open, Huxley gasped, "It's not a garrote, Martha!"

"The things you say, Huxley. What lured you up here tonight?" Martha murmured as she moved around Huxley and tried perfecting the knot a second time.

"I'm here for the fireworks." Huxley answered with an impish grin.

"Fireworks?" I asked.

Bennett chimed in, "Fireworks, Smythe? Perhaps mistletoe flambé?"

Smiling like a keeper of privileged information, Huxley replied, "I heard Martha's all fired up. Might go off like a Roman candle....again!!"

Martha barked, "Huxley you're the biggest gossip in the Valley! Don't believe everything you hear."

I couldn't help myself. "Martha, have you been misbehaving?" I needled.

"You people need to get a life. There, Hux." She let go of the tie.

Dr. Walter Klyce was the next to join our little group. He's an Olana board member and very handsome in a sort of Robert Duvall way.

Smiling he said, "Evening, Huxley, Bennett. Surrounded by adoring women, as always. Your usual two glasses, I see, Lindsey. Martha, have you calmed down?"

Martha snatched her glass from me and smiled, "Everything is under control, Dr. Klyce."

I hate being in the dark. "Calmed down from what? What's under control?"

"Nothing to get excited about," Martha muttered tersely. "Sheila and I had a little run-in at the Board meeting the other day. That's all."

Klyce continued, "Well, you seemed pretty excited. You know Martha when she doesn't get her way. Hey, Bill!"

William van der Wyck, Olana's curator, sleek in an exceptionally vivid scarlet tartan smoking jacket joined us. Placing his arm around her, he said, "Martha is my ally in all things Olana and I support her *every* desire! Her command is my wish! Thank you all so much for coming. Look at this crowd! I think this may turn out to be the most exciting Christmas party we've ever had."

Huxley cried out, "Honoria! Darling!" and we turned to greet Honoria Beekman, Huxley's contemporary, walking toward the group in an ancient ecru evening gown and ermine stole. Honoria is a regal dowager from Charleston whose bearing reflects her Southern gentility and her status as having married into the Beekmans, the oldest and most prominent family in the Hudson Valley.

"Honoria!" Huxley kissed her hand. "Our Chatelaine! How lovely you look!"

Honoria inclined her head toward each of us in turn and offered a few words. "I just cannot believe all these people—what a crowd! William, they must be here to see your red jacket. Lindsey, you look marvelous. Huxley, I haven't seen you since Appomattox---but you never seem to age."

"MY portrait's in the attic, dear!" Hux answered.

Honoria continued. "Bennett, we thoroughly enjoyed that lemon cake you brought over--delicious! Martha, you look well. Do you have a date tonight?" Martha is Honoria's niece.

"Not exactly." Martha glanced around as if looking to see if, indeed, she did have a date.

"What does THAT mean!?" Huxley roared. "Do you or don't you?"

Martha answered, "I think I'm supposed to be here with someone but ...." Martha's voice trailed off. She lifted her glass in a vague gesture. "How are you, Aunt Honoria? Where's Uncle Robert?"

"He stayed by the fire like a sensible human," Honoria smiled. "Told me to keep an eye on things, not to let anything untoward happen tonight."

Bennett was amused. "*Untoward?* At *this* party? You must be joking!"

Honoria shook her head. "It's strange, but we always seem to have some disaster at this party. Like the Christmas that baby fell into the punch bowl. Fell right in! You remember, Lindsey. You fished the little thing out. How we escaped having the entire table refinished I will never know. William, the house looks grand. It's a big evening for you---and your cohort. Where is Sheila?"

"Yes, where is Sheila?" I asked.

William replied curtly, "Probably slavering over Lucius, our newest donor."

Huxley asked, "Do I detect a note of professional friction?"

William answered softly, "You detect loathing, Huxley. Low-grade, to be sure, but loathing."

"Which one is Lucius?" Bennett asked.

William gestured to a handsome fellow across the room, tall and elegant, with wavy silver hair and an attractive silver beard. He was holding forth to an attentive clutch of admirers, mostly women. He wore half spectacles, gray flannels, a midnight blue jacquard jacket and matching waistcoat, a red pattern foulard at a rakish angle, and evening slippers.

"Over there. Hmm. Don't see Sheila. Alas, she'll turn up, just when you least expect--or want her. Well, if you all will excuse me, it's---as they say---showtime!"

William van der Wyck, as Olana's curator, our host for the evening, mounted the stairs to the landing as the musicians gathered their lutes, cello, and harp and stepped aside. Someone began tapping on a glass, as if to make a toast, and the crowd became quiet. People in the dining room and study pressed into the living room for a better view of the evening's main event.

Looking out over the crowd and smiling broadly, Bill clapped his hands a few times and began to speak.

"Good evening one and all, and Merry Christmas! It's wonderful to see so many of you here. I want to share this evening's tributes with my colleague, Sheila Marks. Sheila!" he called. "Where are you, darling? Sheila?" Many of the evening's heads turned, looking one way and another, but no one appeared.

"Well, she seems not to be here at the moment, probably attending to some important detail elsewhere. So let's go forward!" he cried. "The excitement has been building and I know all of you are keen to see the marvelous new canvas which has been brought to us by a mystery donor. We'll tell you about the painting when it is unveiled---and introduce our gracious donor---but I can tell you now," William exuberantly flung out his arms, "it is unlike any other Church work and it is going to stand art historians on their ears!

"And now, I give you, the newest Frederic Church painting!"

With a flourish, he swept aside the drapery to reveal a painting very definitely unlike any other Church canvas: A dark-haired beauty in a white cotton dress, unbuttoned to the waist, and parted to reveal her breasts.

But what caught everyone's eye was beside the painting.

13

Another nude, the director of Olana, Sheila Marks, suspended by a rope around her neck and hanging absolutely still.

AND SO IT BEGINS

When the phone rang at seven the next morning, I was not surprised to hear Paul Whitbeck, the County Sheriff .

"Hey. Pretty grim last night."

"Absolutely terrible," I replied.

"Don't suppose you'd like to come out of retirement and give your old pal the Sheriff a hand on this? Ex-officio, of course."

"Oh, Paul. When did we meet?"

"About twenty years ago. In the city."

"And was I a cop? Was I investigating murders?"

"No, you were helping us investigate art and antique heists, and just a smidge of smuggling. That's not too far from murder, is it?"

"It's quite far, dear Sheriff."

"Not so far. This murder had a portrait. And a house full of art connoisseurs. All of which you know more about than I do. Especially the crowd. Someone at the party did it, Lindsey. You could help me cover a lot of ground quick-like. I know you like a good case. And I know you're good to have on a case."

"I don't know.......I don't know..."

"And bring me some decent coffee." He hung up.

Before leaping out of bed, I permitted myself a long, loud, "Yessssssss!"

I quickly flew through my Laszlo, filled a thermos, and pulled on cords, a well-worn jacket and boots and drove downtown. The winter morning was stunningly clear, pure white sunshine, the mountains purple and taupe silhouettes against the bright blue sky.

Locals still call the road into town the Bay Road because it is actually a causeway traversing what used to be the harbor when Hudson was a whaling port.

Sheriff Paul Whitbeck is from Hudson, enlisted in the Marines out of high school, then went to Fordham, joining the NYPD after graduation and eventually becoming a detective. His curious habit of spouting aphorisms, many of which are malaprops, gives people the idea he's a dim bulb, but he isn't. He sometimes behaves like a bumpkin when it serves his purpose.

He and I met in New York years ago when he was investigating an art theft on the Upper East Side and I was called in to consult. Eventually he tired of city life, took early retirement, came back here to help manage his family's apple farm, then ran for Sheriff.

On a blistering August day shortly after I moved up, I ran into Paul rummaging around in the same pile of white corn I was pawing through at a truck stand and we instantly renewed our friendship. Paul's weathered face is ruggedly handsome with a bristly moustache and graying brown hair that often needs a trim. In the winter he always wears starched flannel shirts with jackets even more ancient than mine and knit ties like my father used to wear. He has beautiful, strong hands.

Paul began this morning's meeting by producing two mugs, thanking me for the coffee as he unscrewed the thermos, and proffering half of his bear claw.

I asked what he knew about the murder victim.

"Sheila Marks was a local girl, married a local boy who became a lawyer and got his name on the door early in his practice. He would have taken over the firm had he not gotten his fingers firmly wrapped around a bourbon bottle. This was maybe fifteen years ago. No kids."

I asked, "Husband still around?"

"He's down the hall. We collected him in the wee hours this morning. Said he'd been at a roadhouse up in Valatie the better part of the evening and was at home sleeping it off. We pumped him full of breakfast an hour ago so he's reasonably sober and awake now. Let's go talk to him."

"Are you charging him?" I asked.

"Not yet."

We went down the narrow, gray hall, past bulletin boards of wanted posters and missing juvenile flyers to the holding room. Ted Marks must have been a gorgeous guy when he was younger. A bit over six feet tall with the build of a runner, shaggy black hair flecked with gray. But his features had flattened, the shoulders had slumped. He wore a look of bored resignation and a suit that had been slept in.

Pulling up a chair, Paul said, "I've asked Lindsey to sit in, Ted, if that's all right with you. She was at the party last night and may be able to shed some light on things."

I spoke first. "Ted, I'm terribly sorry about Sheila."

He said only, "Right."

Paul picked up with the standard interrogatory.

"Why would anybody want to do that to your wife?"

Ted shook his head.

"You weren't at the party?" Paul asked, sifting through a manila folder on the table.

"Why would I go? It was her scene. Meet and greet the money people. Schmooze. Act the part."

"What does that mean?"

"It means that some point, my wife disappeared. A social figurine replaced her. It means she got into Olana as a secretary, worked constantly at her new calling until she wound up running the place. That job was her whole life---and there was really nothing left for me. If I'd been a banker, instead of a failed country lawyer, maybe I'd have gotten some attention.

But as it is, she didn't need me and, to be frank, I didn't have a hell of a lot of need for her." He trailed off. No tears.

I asked, "You didn't want to go to her party --- so you had one of your own?"

"You bet. I was at the Post Road Inn. Having a few. Having another few. Ask around. It's an alibi, in case you decide that I need one."

According to the doctor at the scene---the medical examiner was stuck in a blizzard in Rochester and wouldn't be back for the autopsy until tomorrow at the earliest---the time of death was estimated at late afternoon, which meant she'd been killed shortly before the party.

"What I can't figure out," Paul said, sipping the last of his coffee, "is the timing. People were all over that place from morning getting ready for the party. But somehow she must have been hanged right there on the landing. No one could have waltzed in with a body under his arm."

Paul looked out the window that was covered with heavy wire in a diamond pattern. "We'll have to check out the Post Road Inn. You ever been there?"

"Can't say that I have. It's that place on the way to Stuyvesant, right? Looks dingy. Doesn't seem like his kind of place."

"Well, we're going to need to check his story. But first I thought we'd go back over to Olana. When you called me last night I could hardly hear you so many people were screaming and we barely spoke after I got there."

I nodded. "A lot of people were very frightened. Two fainted. Last thing in the world anyone expected to see was a body at the end of a rope. Glad you got there as fast as you did. The emergency guys were quick, too, and got everybody out in an orderly way. Still, it was a tough night."

"Sheila's assistant and the staff are waiting for us. Why don't you ride with me? I'll have one of our guys bring your car."

As we got our coats and headed out to Paul's Jeep, he remarked on the new county office building we could see under construction a block away.

"God, I'll be glad when we move in. I'll have every modern convenience. Wireless reception. New forensics lab. New morgue. Cappuccino machine. Can't wait."

"Remind me. What was there before?"

"You remember -- it was a junkyard. Been there for at least 150 years. Had old Packards, cannons, pieces of the first telephones ever made. An electric cable Edison strung personally. Eight generations of junkyard magnates made a living off the scrap metal. But the latest crop became accountants and sold the old place off. You were here when they made the movie, right?"

A Depression-era tearjerker was filmed on Columbia Street a few years back. The street was so unchanged from the 1930s, all the set designer had to do was spread dirt over the pavement and bring in old cars, buckboards, and mules and you'd have sworn you'd stepped into a time warp.

I opined, "This must've been a hell of a town back then."

Paul nodded and began to rehearse the town's history for me. Again.

Favorite tales love retelling.

"Quakers settled us in 1662. In 1785, Hudson was the first chartered city in New York. We became a whaling port led by families from Nantucket and Cape Cod who wanted to whale in peace without worrying about the British. Back then this was called Diamond Street. It was famous! Famous! The largest red light district on the eastern seaboard! Prostitution put Hudson on the map!

"It started during the Revolutionary War. The Brits needed to supply women to their troops, so they rounded up a bunch of gals who liked the neighborhood so well they stayed. And believe you me, Hudson made it worth their while! Prostitution, gambling, illegal whiskey -- what a scene! In 1951, Tom Dewey was making a name for himself so he staged a raid. Caught half the police force in the whorehouses. After that, the town fathers, who had been turning a blind eye for more than a hundred years, finally cleaned it up. They even changed the name. No more Diamond Street. Since then it's been Columbia Street.

"When I was a little kid," Paul reminisced, "I'd sit around with my grandfather who'd tell me---a kid!---the most extraordinary tales. Floating crap games with the jailer as the dealer, the mayor running out the back door of a pleasure house and his wife after him with a shotgun. Wild times, let me tell you." Paul laughed. "The madams would pay Gramps a dime to go on beer runs or to stand lookout for the cops. Gramps said a lot of the women were nicer to him than his own relatives, particularly during the Thirties when money was so scarce. Lots of times the girls would feed him dinner or send him home with a covered dish and a dollar. Nice women."

"So what happened to the girls of ill repute?" I asked.

"Most of them found husbands, joined the respectable ranks, raised daughters and sons and put their colorful past behind them. Once a couple of generations had passed, nobody remembered your grandma's name used to be 'Easy Lil.' "

When we arrived at Olana, two groundskeepers were shoveling away snow that had fallen overnight and salting the brick stairs and walkway leading from the parking lot.

The sun shone brilliantly this morning. The shrubs and grounds around the house were glazed with ice, the evergreens under a blanket of white. Heading up to the house, we passed a pocket garden fenced with thick, gnarled wild grape vines. In summer, banana trees flourished there as they would have in Victorian 1876 when the house was new. Olana's view extended almost fifty miles south --- and, were there no intervening hills, on a clear day one could see the skyline of Manhattan. To the west, three ranges of the Catskills and Adirondacks rose majestically. To the east, foothills of the Berkshires were dark blue against the matte gold of winter fields edged by hemlocks and pines.

Although I have visited Olana countless times, I am always astonished when I see it---I expect everyone is. Every aspect of the house is so literally fantastic, and so incongruous---a Moorish citadel surveying this epitome of American landscapes.

As he set about designing a home, Frederic Edwin Church originally envisioned a French-style chateau at the summit of the property. But in 1867, shortly after he had accumulated the 260 acres of farmland just south of Hudson, Church, with his wife and infant son, embarked on an eighteen-month tour of the Holy Lands---Damascus, Jerusalem, Palestine, Beirut, the lost city of Petra---and the trip changed the artist's sensibilities forever. Church's newfound fascination with Persian art and architecture transformed his vision of the house he would build.

Olana bristles with Moorish towers, turrets, and loggias. The great walls of the house are built from light brown stone quarried on the property but are embellished with miles of colorful ornate brickwork and elaborate tiled patterns on cornices, windows, balconies, and roofs. The house has the grandeur of a castle and the ornament of an Arabian wedding chest.

Rounding the corner, we came to the front of the house with its intricately tiled portico and ceramic plaque above the massive doorway reading Olana, from the Arabic, 'place on high.' Below us, the river curled southward like a silver ribbon, winding and turning in the sunshine.

Paul and I kicked our boots against the bluestone porch steps to shed snow and stepped inside.

The house's exterior promises mystery and enchantment and its interior does not disappoint. Named for a fortress treasure house in the Middle East, Olana's rooms overflow with exotic objects from Church's travels---painted Kashmiri tables with mother-of-pearl and silver inlay, pre-Columbian relics, mounted birds and butterflies, bronze and marble statuary. The floors and grand staircase are covered in Persian carpets. Elaborate stencils in muted reds, coppers, greens, and golds border each door and window. The house is extraordinary and exciting. Every visit is an adventure---but none before like the preceding night's dreadful spectacle.

My eyes had just begun to adjust to the muted light within the house when I heard my name being called from outside.

Manny Feller, the head groundsman, beckoned to me. Waving Paul on, I stepped back onto the portico.

"Greetings of the season, young Feller," said I familiarly, having had occasion to hire Manny for odd jobs at my house over the years. Manny, who has to be 75 if he's a minute, wore two parkas with hoods and heavy work pants, all covered in a rough canvas insulated jump suit, leather gloves, and black rubber boots to his knees.

"Happy Christmas to you, Miss Lindsey," he said as we embraced. "I hope you'll put in a good word for me when you find the time is right."

"A good word for you about what?"

"Now she's dead, it may not matter, but she was going to fire me. I don't know if she talked about it with anybody else, but I'm hoping now she's out of the way—what I mean is, now that she's passed on, maybe there won't be no more talk about my leaving on to it."

"Why would anybody in her right mind even consider getting rid of you, Manny? Heavens, you've been the main man around here almost since Mr. Church himself was in the house. I expect the place would fall down if you weren't looking after things."

"You may say so but you ain't the boss here, Miss Lindsey. The years I spent plowing and sanding this drive, ditching with a shovel when we didn't have no backhoe on to it, clearing brush, mowing every week in summer so the lilac didn't cover the whole place. Lived here two weeks straight in '85, never even went home, when that October snow we got took down a thousand trees. She wasn't the Queen then. Now she says we need somebody who knows Latin plant names or some damn thing on to it, as if that makes any difference to the grounds or the weather. Don't nobody take better care of this place and get the flowers and beds to bloom better than I do and I'm not sorry to say that to her face even if she is dead."

Manny, who is known for his sunny disposition, looked dour and grizzled. I slipped a crisp fifty into his pocket and said, "When it comes time to say something good about you, I'll know it and I'll say it. By the way, why did you decide to hang her instead of just using your trusty twelve gauge?"

I laughed at my joke, but Manny swore.

"Don't think I'm not expecting to have fingers pointed at me, by God," he said, and turned away.

The hastily abandoned tables, glasses, and serving platters for the party, like so many still lifes, remained where they had been the night before. Several of Paul's officers moved slowly through the rooms examining every surface looking for something to shed light on Sheila's death. I couldn't imagine how they would separate hundreds of innocent guests' fingerprints from the one smudge that might be actual evidence.

The portrait stood, unlit, on the left side of the landing and I walked closer. It was a tender portrait of a very beautiful woman. There were definitely flourishes characteristic of Church. The bare-breasted woman---hardly more than a girl, really---was framed by a sultry, tropical landscape and ancient ruins. I turned away and walked through the house's front parlor and central court, then turned sharply down a narrow stair descending to the lower floor that had been the servants' quarters and kitchen.

Olana's upstairs rooms are exactly as they were in the 19th century. The downstairs has been converted to a warren of unremarkable, taupe carpeted not-for-profit offices. Walls are painted pale dill and hung with photographs of the house and grounds taken throughout the seasons. Filing cabinets line the corridors between offices. There was a Xerox room with a huge photocopier, a water cooler, coffee machines, postage meter and scales, office supplies, and back issues of publications.

I found Paul sitting at Sheila's desk.

"There's nothing whatsoever personal," Paul said, gesturing with his hand around the room as I sat down in front of him. "These photos of Sheila with a lot of people I don't recognize, except the Governor, all this is work stuff. I glanced through her desk, nothing immediately pops out. This one drawer is locked. I'll have someone go through her other files." He leaned forward and picked up an open desk calendar. "This shows two appointments in the next week. One's with a Lucius Wrangel. Doesn't say where. And there's an appointment two days after Christmas in New York City with a Dr. Wishman. East 86th.

Looking around the room, I found myself trying to conjure an image, a personality for the victim. The bookshelves contained Who's Who, the New York social register, back issues of Avenue Magazine and Vanity Fair, as well as New York, Albany, and Boston telephone directories and the Directory of Philanthropy. Two shelves held stacks of companies' annual reports. Standard development tools, to be expected.

"Her assistant, Eve Healy is waiting for us. I thought we'd talk to her, the Head Docent---a woman named Spriggins---and Van der Wyck, the curator. I've got the boys going over everything upstairs. This Eve person was with Sheila all day yesterday. She'll be able to give us an account of what went on. Maybe she'll have the key to the desk, too."

Sheila's assistant, Eve Healy, was waiting in her office two doors down. She was standing at the window looking out at the carriage house and turned to greet us. Like Sheila, Eve had blond hair, but hers was long and pulled back with a ribbon. She had blue eyes, and was attractive in a quiet way. She and Sheila looked enough alike to be sisters, except while Sheila had been petite, Eve was basketball material---very trim, but almost six feet tall. As if to understate her good looks, she wore an olive drab tweed suit and a simple white blouse.

We all sat down.

"How long have you worked here?" Paul asked.

"Almost ten years," she answered. "I was originally hired to work the ticket window and help with record-keeping. When Sheila found I was good with computers, she promoted me to the membership office, and I helped with mailings, fund solicitations. I became her executive assistant several years ago. As all of her hard work paid off, Olana had more and more events and fundraisers. Sheila needed to spend more time cultivating donors and left the day-to-day business to me. She was Miss Outside, I was Miss Inside."

I asked, "What did your day-to-day entail exactly?"

"Scheduling the docents, managing the maintenance staff, dealing with contractors, supervising the gift store, going to the bank."

"Making deposits?"

"Yes---from memberships, contributions, the gift store, and admissions fees." She shifted in her chair and pulled at the collar of her tweed jacket.

"How much money are we talking about?" Paul asked.

"When I began the admissions fees were laughable---two dollars, three dollars. And we didn't sell anything except postcards. Sheila converted the carriage house into a gift store and raised admissions fees to $10. We also charge a five dollar entrance fee per car, even if people don't tour the house.

"The grounds are open all year but our season really begins in early spring when the trees are just starting to leaf. April. That's when the house opens to visitors. We usually get upwards of 75,000 people a year."

"So at ten bucks a pop, plus the car fees, that's close to a million," Paul said. "What about the gift shop?"

"People mostly buy picture frames and cards, maybe a trivet or a book. Some of the books are expensive. We also have kilim pillows and the type of Persian rugs Mr. Church had in the house. The rugs can be pricey. Usually it's about $1000 a week, but we have hit $10,000. But that's just in summer and later in the fall when we are overrun with leaf peepers. Olana is in all the guidebooks to the Valley, of course---we're a must-see. We usually make a night deposit at the end of each day. If not every day, the receipts are kept in the safe."

"You have the combination, of course. And who else" Paul asked.

"Sheila did."

"How will things be different without Sheila?" I asked.

Eve produced a starched handkerchief and dabbed her eyes, although I had not noticed tears. She answered, "We're all still in shock, of course. I can't imagine who would've wanted to kill her. She was doing such a great job."

"I'm not sure a favorable performance review had much to do with it," I observed. "How did she get on with the staff?"

"Beautifully. We all loved her and her dedication to Olana and the plans she had for making it even greater."

"Who'll be taking over her position?" Paul asked. "Will you be promoted?"

Eve shrugged. "That's certainly not for me to say. It's up to the board. Naturally, I'd want to do whatever the board asked me to do. If they asked."

"Were you and Sheila close? You know, drinks after work? Lunches, that sort of thing?"

"Not really," she said. "Most of her time was spent with donors or the board."

"Tell us what you were doing the day of the party."

"I checked several times to make sure the outside walkways and stairs had all been cleared and salted. We had a new caterer who'd never worked here before so I had to make sure they had what they needed and put their staging areas and equipment in the right place. I supervised the wine delivery. I confirmed all the docents were on hand. At about five, I came down here and dressed in my office."

"When did you last see Sheila?"

"She and Helen Spriggins came down here just as I was going to the powder room to freshen my makeup. When I came back here to put away my cosmetics, she was not in her office. I assumed she had gone back upstairs."

"What was she wearing when you saw her?"

"Just jeans and a turtleneck. She hadn't changed for the party yet."

"Thank you, Eve," Paul said. "We'll be in and out for the next several days and will be in touch." said Paul, standing.

"Oh---I almost forgot. One of the drawers in Sheila's desk is locked. Do you have the key?"

"To Sheila's desk? I'm not sure. I have a lot of extra keys somewhere. I'll check and let you know."

Paul handed her his card. "Call me when you find it."

WHAT THE DOCENT SAW

We set up in the Olana employees' lunchroom for our next interview with Mrs. Helen Spriggins, Olana's head docent. Paul and I stood as a young patrolman ushered Mrs. Spriggins in.

Mrs. Spriggins' abundant bosom appeared adequate to topple her short frame had her spine not been made of titanium. She was encased in a medium gray gabardine suit of some vintage with a white silk blouse knotted in a flounce at her throat, the requisite pearls, and a brooch on her lapel.

"Shall I sit here?" she asked in an imperious tone.

"Yes, please," Paul answered, straightening his tie.

"Why are we in here?" she demanded. "Surely the upstairs rooms are more suitable. Or even an actual office."

The Formica tables offended her.

"Upstairs is probably more comfortable but as we are searching all the rooms …"

"For a weapon?!" Mrs. Spriggins interjected. "What have you learned so far? I assume you will be bringing in the FBI. You must feel out of your depth."

Paul answered, "I assure you we are in the process of finding Sheila's killer, Mrs. Spriggins. And we very much hope you can help us."

"What is *she* doing here?" Mrs. Spriggins demanded, casting a glare in my direction. "Why is she being given special treatment?"

Mrs. Spriggins lives nearby in an early 18th century colonial with the date 1 7 2 8 blazoned across the front. Her house's age confers Mrs. Spriggins' prestige and verifies her feeling of superiority. Unfortunately, her husband, an affable old railroad conductor, never achieved the professional rank required to validate her status absolutely and a deeply dissatisfied Mrs. Spriggins has therefore been in a very bad mood in her very old house for a very long time.

Her haughty reference to my 'special treatment' confirmed what I had long suspected: Mrs. Spriggins doesn't like me.

Why? She has been unable to glean much about me, certainly not about my foibles. Mrs. Spriggins prefers to have others' foibles at her fingertips. And worse, I have no husband, but do have a butler. Very worrisome to Mrs. Spriggins.

"Lindsey is offering her assistance in determining how the crime might have been committed and by whom. She was there last night, as you know."

"I was not aware the murder had been committed with an antique, which I am given to understand is Ms. Brooks' *only* area of expertise. I, too, was at the party," announced Mrs. Spriggins in ominous tones. "I saw the woman. She was hanged."

As Paul was inhaling, I sprang in. "Exactly! Which," I hurried on, "is precisely why it is most important we speak to you immediately, Mrs. Spriggins. Helen," I said gravely, "your powers of observation are impeccable. Please tell us what you saw and heard last evening."

"I am the *Head* Docent," Mrs. Spriggins began, drawing up herself up. The buttons of the gray gabardine strained, but held.

"I am responsible for absolute authenticity in all house narratives. At the Christmas party, docent recitations illuminate the symbolism and significance of holiday décor, many details of which derive from Mrs. Church's diaries.

"Last night, all docents presented themselves at 4:45 sharp to be given their final room assignments. Each of us wore a corsage. During the party, as guests tour the house, we are stationed at the portal of each room, offering rich, historical information and engaging anecdotes about Yuletides past and the provenance of decorations and furnishings.

"Was Sheila there when you were rehearsing the docents?" Paul asked.

"Sheila made her presence felt throughout the afternoon as she and Eve supervised the caterers' chaotic arrival and staging, the placement of the musicians, verification of guest lists, and other housekeeping details."

"Where had you stationed yourself?"

"As Head Docent, I was to be in the dining room wherein the decorations reach their zenith. This year, the ferns, the plumes, the orchids..." She cast another glare in my direction.

"Stupendous!" I exploded.

Satisfied, Helen continued. "As I was admiring the dining room, I heard Sheila and Dr. Van der Wyck's voices across the hall. I went to them seeking confirmation on details of certain of the old masters in the dining room. I'm sure you know Mr. Church often retouched others' paintings to improve them."

Here Mrs. Spriggins leaned forward and continued *sotto voce*. "To my horror, I walked in on an extremely unpleasant confrontation. William and Sheila were locked in a pitched battle about the evening's program.

"Van der Wyck was obviously furious! I heard him swear at Sheila. He said, 'Damn you! We're going to settle this once and for all,' and he grabbed her arm as if to drag her from the room or strike her. Sheila pulled away and said, 'It *is* settled. Now get the hell away from me! Go and curate something.'

"At that moment, they both realized I was watching them. Sheila quickly took my arm and asked me to accompany her downstairs. She and I left hastily as Van der Wyck continued to rage, saying the most unpleasant things. Sheila was still in jeans and told me her clothes for the party were in her car, that she had to get them and dress. She pulled on her gloves, threw on a muffler and left by the back downstairs door."

"Did you see her after that?"

"I don't believe I did."

"What time would that have been?"

"Shortly after five o'clock. I remember telling her she should dress quickly because guests would be coming any minute and the painting hadn't even arrived yet."

"What happened to Van der Wyck?"

"I returned to the dining room to query Dr. Van der Wyck on the retouching but that proved impossible given his turbulent behavior. He was still agitated and pacing in the upstairs hall. I heard him say, 'Damn it, I've had enough of this.' Then he walked out and slammed the front door. He obviously intercepted her and killed her. I think you should arrest him."

Paul said, "But there's a Catch 23 about that."

His malaprops were new to Mrs. Spriggins. She leaned toward him. "A what?"

"A Catch 23. Van der Wyck went outside when Sheila went to her car, but Manny Feller, the groundsman, tells me the two men ran headlong into each other on the front porch. Van der Wyck wound up helping Feller replace a flood light. By the time that was finished, Wrangel and the van and crew bringing the painting arrived and Van der Wyck had to supervise the porters bringing the portrait in and setting it up."

"Arrest them all," directed Mrs. Spriggins.

32

A VISIT TO THE BEEKMANS

Leaving Paul and his crew to finish interviewing the staff and combing the grounds, I called Honoria and Robert Beekman and asked for a cup of tea. Honoria has sharp eyes and might have noticed something unusual the night before. The Beekmans live in the last of the family-owned Beekman manor houses up here. At one point their family owned five estates along the river and had a patent for 200,000 acres, a gift from James II who saw them as loyal subjects in the colonies.

Over time, inter-marriage---Beekmans truly care only for *other* Beekmans---had, shall we say, diminished the gene pool. Ill-advised investments, estate taxes, and simple sloth had reduced the family's real estate to this final manor, Locust Mount. It had never been the most beautiful of the Beekman houses and the unfortunate modification of a Mansard roof in the late 1800s had further corrupted its lines. From a distance, the house looked like a large, beige breadbox.

The interior, however, was quite another story. In my earlier career running Garnier Luxe Art and Antiques (galleries and halls in New York, Paris, and Geneva), we had approached the Beekmans every few years about parting with something from their astonishing hoard of American and English treasures.

For our Masters of Silver show, I spent an extremely long afternoon plying Honoria and Robert with Champagne and foie gras in an effort to persuade them to de-accession one their seven tea services, all of great historical importance and monstrous value. No dice. It has always struck me odd that people would prefer to contend with an unheated kitchen on the back porch and mean temperatures of 58° in the rest of the house rather than part with a tiny portion of their patrimony. Pride goeth before pneumonia.

The artistry and craftsmanship of the antiques, artifacts, and paintings in Locust Mount always give me intense pleasure. Today, arm in arm with Honoria in a long-sleeved Liberty navy print dress, I strolled through the front parlors, stopping to admire various pieces. My fingers brushed the top of an exceptional Pembroke table. A pair of Rembrandt Peale portraits hung above a 17th century Virginia sugar chest. Broad black ribbons suspended three Bierstadts and a Cole above a Chippendale sideboard. A fountain pen and notepaper lay upon an early Federal escritoire given the family by George Washington for valor in battle. These beautiful things and many more stood on sixteen-inch-wide plank floors burnished over two hundred years to a deep golden sheen.

"I'm behaving like I'm in a museum, Honoria," I said, giving her arm a squeeze.

"Might as well. No sense asking what's new."

Robert Beekman, Honoria's husband of sixty-odd years ambled in. Throwing his arms wide, he announced, "I was promised tea! Lindsey, give me a hug!"

Honoria said, "The tray is over here, Robert. Come on, Lindsey. Let's sit down. You're wearing me out looking at my own house."

Honoria and I sank into a pair of Queen Anne chairs upholstered during Roosevelt's third term, with Robert on a settee opposite us across the tea table. As warm December sunshine streamed through the big windows, Honoria poured and we began to speak of the previous evening at Olana.

I broached the subject.

"Last night was ghastly."

Honoria groaned, her forehead furrowed in pain. She leaned forward, then rocked back, eyes closed, shaking her head.

"It was astonishing. I've never seen anything so terrible. That poor girl. I'm just thankful the children"--- her grandchildren---"weren't there. We'll all have nightmares until we go to our graves, I know I will."

Robert sipped his tea and looked relaxed in a gray cardigan, white shirt, rep tie and gray slacks. In his early nineties now, Robert remains a very handsome man, although he is somewhat diminished not only by age, but unfortunately by the insidious tendrils of early dementia.

He observed, "I can't understand how she got up there."

"Well, Robert," I replied, "obviously she was hanged."

"Last time I heard of that was during the war when the British made a special trip up the river to Beaumont, my great-great-great-great uncle's place down the road. When they couldn't find him, they hanged several of the staff. As a special gesture, we buried them near the family plot."

"Robert," I smiled, "I seriously doubt Sheila's hanging was the work of the British navy.

"Honoria," I asked, "you were at the house earlier that day giving the Christmas decorations a last look. How did Sheila seem to you? Was she nervous? Distracted in any way?"

"No more nervous than anyone would be before three hundred people tramped through an old house you were preserving for posterity," said Honoria, her eyebrows arched.

"*Of course* she seemed distracted, Lindsey! Any sane person *would* be distracted, worrying about a replay of some previous year's disaster. And not just that poor baby in the punch bowl. Do you remember the year that man put the épergne on his head? In 1990, the year the snow was so bad, someone hit a pole on the Bay Road and all the lights went out for twenty minutes. When they came back on, two people I had never seen before were under the piano and I hardly need to tell you what *they* were up to, surely." Honoria's eyes widened for emphasis.

"Yes," she went on, "I dare say any intelligent person would have been preoccupied.

"And, of course, I'm sure she felt the added concern of this big new donor being there, peering around and staring at us to see if we measured up enough for him to deign to join the board." Honoria sighed.

I asked, "Who exactly was that?"

"Well, I don't know him, of course, but I gather his family practically owned Russia. Old nobility. And he apparently owns Wall Street. You should ask Martha. She's the one who got him up here and worked him over about Olana in the first place. In addition, if anything suspicious happened last night, Martha would have spotted it. Call her right now. Have her give you lunch."

Martha Lee is Honoria's late sister's child. I've known Martha for thirty years and can attest she is the poster child of the poor little rich girl. Her father patented the light switch and then went on to invent Teflon. Every time anyone in the world turns on a lamp or flips an omelet, Martha makes a quarter. Martha is addicted to ice cream and gay men; one is endlessly fattening, the other endlessly flattering because Martha picks up all the checks. She is eccentric, colorful, very bright, more than a trifle overweight, and the most garrulous person I have ever met.

Martha lives on the other side of the river and, as the winter day continued fine, I crossed the Rip Van Winkle bridge. Beneath me, on an island, trees' charcoal fingers stretched toward a cloudless blue sky and two barges plowing northward negotiated heavy ice in the river.

If you have been thinking of looking at real estate in upstate New York, Martha's town, Concentration, is a good place to get a bargain. The West Bank of the Hudson has never been as prosperous as the East Bank. The little towns peaked, if you can call it that, around the turn-of-the-century. When the Great Depression arrived and stayed, sons and daughters left for city jobs. The market research term for the current population is 'hardscrabble.'

Martha built her house on the outskirts of Concentration, a nondescript hamlet that has over the last twenty years been transformed into an artsy little community, with painters and sculptors from New York buying and rehabbing old farms and barns, or building new houses designed to resemble old houses. From the outside, Martha's place looks to be just a large faux colonial, but I'd term the inside Extreme Bunny Bower. Lots of chintz, old Persians, Henredon rabbits, Boehme birds, magnificent silver and china, and enough freeze-dried eucalyptus to make a koala wince. It looks like a branch of James Robinson.

Martha greeted me at the door in a chartreuse wool challis muumuu over gray slacks, a lime green-embroidered lemon vest over that and a fuchsia pashmina scarf topping off the ensemble. The entire effect was so colorful I felt my retinas trembling.

"Can you stand it?!?" Martha shrieked, pulling me through the foyer and into the living room. "We've had a murder! I ran like a rabbit last night! Tell me everything you know so far and don't skip over the good parts."

"We don't know a hell of a lot as yet," I said, taking a seat in a persimmon wing chair, moving a pillow needle-pointed with the family crest. "Sheila was dead when the party started, obviously. We won't have the full forensic report for a day or maybe two. Honoria said Sheila was nervous about some large wallet you had lured onto the scene. Who is that?"

"That would be Lucius Wrangel. He's new up here. I met him at 21, totally by chance, in the lobby bar. His date was late. Mine got lucky and never showed. I sat down beside him and my charisma took over. He said he was looking for land up here, took me up on my invitation to show him around. Lucius figured out that Olana is the fastest way to meet anybody important. First he gifted the house with a tiny little Sanford Gifford, then with a Thomas Cole sketch, then fifty thou. They're voting for him to be on the board next month."

"So he knew Sheila? She had pursued him for the Board?" I asked.

"Of course! She did her usual unctuous number when she met him, which seems, or seemed, I should say, to charm almost everybody. Underneath all that veneer, she was just a babe with pretensions, but it worked. Must've been the blond hair."

"I had no idea you were so close."

"She had no use for women at all and since it was my family's money that got Olana fund-raising off the ground in the first place, I thought she could have been friendlier. I don't mean that she wasn't friendly. She was über-friendly, but *so* transparent. I don't care for people who act like someone they aren't."

Martha abruptly jumped up. "I'm going to get us something, what do you want? You just left Aunt Honoria and Uncle Robert so we can forget tea. How about a sherry? Or I've got a really good Gavi. Let's do that."

Martha bustled off to the kitchen and I heard cabinets opening and the refrigerator door closing.

"Here," she said, coming back holding the glasses in one hand by their stems and the wine in her other, pulling at the half-out cork with her teeth. "Gif thus outf," she mumbled.

I took the bottle, pulled out the cork and poured.

"Where were we?" she asked.

"Country girl comes up in world, woos nouveaux riches. So she was a pretender?" I asked.

"Exactly. The way she acted, you'd have thought she was a Beekman herself, when in fact, her father worked at a flour mill and her mother took in sewing," Martha snorted. She lit cigarettes for both of us and propped her leopard Belgian shoes on an ottoman.

"You can't really fault her, I suppose. Her job was to get money and she did work the ward, as the expression goes. The minute she met people with any serious loot she'd invite them on a private house tour. Or maybe a *really* private tour, if you get my drift..

"She more or less ignored all the old guard, only interested in the newbies from New York City, most of whom were like her in that they didn't know the difference between Frederic Church and First Presbyterian, but knew prestige when they saw it. Not Lucius, of course. He's a connoisseur. Still, everybody likes to meet the local gentry and historic preservation is the ticket to society up here."

"When did you last see her?"

Martha's reply surprised me. "Oh---so you've heard about that?"

"Heard about what?"

"Last week's board meeting. I was being rotated off the board, another one of her ideas. Rotate older members off, make room for the new blood. At that meeting, she announced her plans to build a visitors' center to the tune of $30 million at the foot of the hill. Wanted to make it a museum unto itself.

"I was not the only naysayer, not by a long shot! Several of us said it was absurd, a silly plan. Olana is a beautiful house, a unique house. Why raise and spend $30 million on a visitors' center strictly to sell more souvenirs? We should be endowing scholarships, protecting the view shed. I told her she was a pompous, empire-building egotist."

"And what else?" I leaned forward.

"I told her she should be stopped and, if nobody else had the guts, I'd do it."

ANTIQUING IN HUDSON

Downtown Hudson has become a Mecca for antiques. At last count, seventy-something dealers are arrayed along the main street in an exceptionally well-preserved assortment of 18th and 19th century buildings. The vernacular architecture has all been freshly painted, lintels replaced, bricks repointed. The merchandise ranges from bric-a-brac to museum-quality pieces, original Bauhaus, Hepplewhite, Edwardian, and Sheridan furniture, to name a few periods, as well as chandeliers, sconces, rare books, porcelain, and art work of every description.

If you can't find something you want in the stores of Warren Street, you are seriously short on imagination. Or cash.

If you are short on oils of your ancestors, however, your worries are over: Hudson has dozens of suitable substitutes. Many a newcomer has embellished walls with store-bought portraits. Their lineage may initially be dubious but they work fine once you hang them up and prescribe their pedigrees.

Warren Street slopes upward from the river for seven blocks, culminating in a town square. There I parked next to my favorite store, Attique, which is famous for its architectural salvage and country furnishings. Attique consists of two weathered gray clapboard houses filled with a vast horde of mantels, panels, doors, brass hardware, and furniture. An array of wrought iron fencing, gates, garden ornaments, and statuary spills out of the store into its rear courtyard and carriage houses. The enterprising young owner also scours South and Latin American capitals for antiques as well as crockery and components of houses. Sacristy panels from Mexico City stand beside iron furniture from sidewalk cafés in Buenos Aires, and bronze bank tables from Caracas. The entire effect is very stimulating if one enjoys, as I do, reclaiming houses, decorating them, and then allowing lucky people to acquire them.

Often when I have finished restoring a house, a loft, or a barn, and am receiving a real estate agent and her clients, I hear that musical phrase, "Oh, we love it. If *only* we could purchase it *exactly* the way it looks now, with all the furniture."

I frown slightly and lean toward them, as if startled by a previously unheard-of idea. I pause for perhaps ten seconds, then reply haltingly, "Well….I *suppose* you could. It would only be… a *little* more."

A girl's got to eat and thus I sustain myself.

Today I was looking for paneling for a client's library, hoping for chestnut.

As I wandered among chandeliers, Mexican lavabos, Spanish rectory tables, and Bolivian urns, whom should I see standing between a sideboard and a small forest of pedestal sinks, but William van der Wyck.

I walked to him and placed my hand on his arm.

"Bill, I'm so terribly sorry about what happened."

Van der Wyck, who hails from a wealthy Chicago family, is every inch the country curator. Smart tweed jackets, impeccable twill or flannel trousers or, in summer, crisp chinos. Immaculate shirts with bright bow ties. He affects a meticulously groomed mustache severe above his lip in contrast to his impossibly bristly eyebrows. These eyebrows knitted as he said, "Oh, hello, Lindsey. How nice to see you. I've just spent a fascinating two hours with the Sheriff who asked me every question known to man about poor, dear, dead Sheila."

"It was dreadful. I'm sure it upset you very much."

"Well, yes," he answered, "it was quite upsetting. The holiday party to which a great many volunteers had given a great deal of time was completely spoiled. That evening the house is always at its best, candles flickering, brass and crystal gleaming. Did you notice the paintings' colors fairly popping off the walls? Church's sunsets---his vivid oranges, blues, and lavenders are never more beautiful than in chiaroscuro.

"The staff and I always look forward to the Christmas party. We can mingle with neighbors and friends accepting compliments. And of course it is an ideal time to cultivate new people and introduce them to Church and the Hudson River School. To invite them to join the Olana community, impress upon them the value of their support. Yes, it was a damn shame."

"To say nothing of a woman being murdered."

"Oh, you think she was murdered? She had such a gift for grandstanding, I felt certain it was suicide."

"William, in fairness, the woman existed solely to attract supporters to the house. *Her* work made *your* work possible."

He sneered. "If she were here and you asked her, 'Sheila, darling, what is your job?' you wouldn't have heard a word about historic preservation or art. You'd have heard about revenues, expansion, and building, building, building. Olana is about honoring a man and a painterly tradition. It's about scholarship, not income from souvenirs. She wanted to build a diorama worthy of Disney at the foot of the hill. Sheila saw her duty as growing her empire and selling trinkets."

"I understand you and Sheila had a row just before the party."

"Ah, yes! The sheriff told me *dear* Mrs. Spriggins divulged she saw Sheila and me going at it. Yes, we had a fight. A terrific scene. I was sick of Sheila's intrusions." Van der Wyck almost slammed down the Portuguese vase he was holding.

"The gorgon informed me I would not be speaking about the painting, said *she* would do it! Originally, I was to do the unveiling, make a few remarks about the work, and then introduce her. She would then introduce Mr. Wrangel, the lovely man who gave it to us. But she wanted the *entire* spotlight. Yes, I was livid! How would you feel?"

"What happened after you helped Manny with his ladder?"

"Thank heavens he noticed that floodlight was out! All we need is someone breaking a leg in the dark. After Manny and I put the ladder back in the carriage house, I was immediately caught up in the delivery of the portrait that *finally* arrived at the 11th hour. Something about a wreck on the Thruway. I ushered Wrangel and the delivery men in, then went directly into the studio to greet a new couple who had come early to discuss a small Jasper Cropsey they want to donate. As it happens, the Cropsey is redundant to our collection. I delicately explained that the painting would bring enough money at auction to provide five-year stipends to a dozen students---young painters, art historians, graduate students of the period. Happily, they agreed. Then I darted into my office to dress, guests began arriving, thence the party and the unveiling. Which, may I say, turned out to be the highlight of the evening in more ways than one.

"You ask if I'm upset by Sheila's murder? Heavens, no. Someone's done us all a favor."

By the time I left Attique—I found the paneling by the way, as well as a pair of superb stone griffins and a marvelous Argentine terrace grouping for another client—it was dark.

Once home, I prepared two vodka martinis straight up, shaking them to waltz time as Dashiell Hammett instructed in *The Thin Man.* Carrying them into the kitchen, I found Bennett peering into the oven.

"Well?" I asked.

"The confits are progressing nicely, Madame," he answered, taking his drink.

"How's our murder going?"

MAY I INTRODUCE THE MAN NEXT DOOR?

I don't believe you and Bennett have been properly introduced.

I live in a stone house that was originally an inn on the old Dutch road into Hudson. The property has several outbuildings, one of which is a sweet little cottage built of the same stone as my house.

Since I bought the property, the cottage has had many different residents. Early on, when there was lots of work to do on the main house, I installed a caretaker, a carpenter, a fine craftsman. Alas, after several years he married and left to raise a family, fortunately after the renovation phase was behind me. I then alternated between caretakers and tenants for several years. First, there was the tiny landscaper who was wonderful in the garden, installing physostigea, several aconites, crocosmia, and a ravishing clematis paniculata *and* creating a compost pile that made me the envy of the county. But, after allowing every pipe in the house to damn near freeze one winter, she was dispatched.

For several happy years after that, I switched to tenants. The cottage was home to a very nice young couple. She commuted to teach at NYU, he did pro bono law work in Albany. They married while in residence---I hosted the reception---and had a child whose first word was 'boat.' Then she was appointed to head a film department in San Francisco. I still miss them.

Their departure occasioned my pondering what sort of help I might need at this stage of my life. I concluded that I needed a butler, preferably part-time. Someone who would invariably be available to serve at dinner parties---it's as hard to get help up here as anywhere, let me tell you. But I saw no need, nor did I want, to have someone underfoot day in and day out. My house is large but Knole it's not. The perfect solution seemed to be a retired butler to be my part-time factotum. Someone to serve, whip up the occasional fricassee, maintain the pool, help in the garden, and generally fulfill the main assignment of tenant or caretaker---to mind the house when I am away---but who could do as he pleased a great deal of the time.

Hoping to find someone who'd appreciate a modest stipend and free lodging to supplement his retirement pension, I contacted the butlers' guild---honestly, what *did* we do before the internet?---and sent in my specs. Occasional butling. Knowledge of horticulture and cuisine. Charming private cottage in scenic rural area. River view.

And Bennett answered the ad. Checking his references, I found both the dukes he'd worked for in England were highly complimentary. Best of all, he had recently moved to New York! No costly cross-pond relocation expenses!

I suggested we interview over lunch at the Carlyle. I always feel so secure there and one wants to set the correct tone with new staff.

Our first meeting went something like this:

I'm looking terrific in a black and white bouclé suit with red piping and a kick pleat and new black patent heels. I am seated in the restaurant and order a glass of Champagne.

One of the best-looking men I have ever seen comes to the table and says, "Miss Brooks?" I think he's going to tell me I have a phone call but after I say, "Yes?" he says, "Bennett Holbrook, Madame."

His credentials were impeccable, his appearance was impeccable, and from that very moment Bennett demonstrated his graceful ability to succeed at that most difficult of tasks---taking care of me.

We scrutinized the menus, my peeking over the top from time to time. Salt and pepper hair brushed back. Subtle tan. Navy pinstripe suit, white shirt, yellow tie. Slight scar running down his left cheek. Perhaps a smidge older than I. Very fit. Beautiful hands.

"I'm thinking of the pheasant," I offered.

"I would not advise the pheasant, Madame."

"Oh? Why?"

"Yesterday it was unsatisfactory and I cannot see how the chef could have improved upon his technique overnight."

"You lunched here yesterday? Why didn't you say so? We could easily have chosen another restaurant."

"This was an extremely convenient choice, Madame. I had come from a late morning squash game and was easily able to return to my rooms upstairs, shower and dress for lunch. Aside from the pheasant, I think you'll find everything to be superb."

"You're staying here?" I am afraid my astonishment was too evident. Bennett smiled. "Yes, Madame. Is that surprising?"

"It seems lavish for a retired person." I winced. "Forgive me. I am afraid I may have misjudged your, ah, circumstances. I mean, you did answer an ad about a job."

Frantic to change the subject, I plowed on with, "Aside from squash, what are you doing with your time? Do you have hobbies?"

Why did I feel like I was on a date? When had I become a nitwit?

"My interests are in tracing heraldic motifs and teaching myself to paint, Madame. I understand your interests are in the realm of antiques, about which I am reasonably conversant having served, as you know, in two magnificent homes in England."

I was flattered. "How did you know that about me?" I had come prepared to offer the usual précis.

"I Googled you, Madame."

After discussing carte du jour options, Bennett masterfully ordered lunch. As we were passing sauce for the poached sea bass, I began to calm down. Handsome men have this effect on all women, I kept telling myself. Just relax.

"Tell me," I simpered, "is that a dueling scar?"

He grinned mischievously. "On occasion I *have* intimated that it is a dueling scar. The truth is I fell out of a crabapple while pruning."

"What occasioned your move to New York? I'd have expected you to choose Dorset or Cornwall or the Scilly Isles for retirement."

"My only child, my son, lives here and wished me to be near him. I was widowed some years ago and I, too, felt a change of scenery might be advantageous. I always imagined that life in New York would be fascinating and glamorous. And it is. But I also yearn for the countryside. That is what attracted me about your employment notice. 'Rural area. River view.'"

By the time we completed the salad course, we were nattering away like old friends. As we approached the midpoint of the second bottle of Meurseult, I framed my awkward question as best I could.

"Bennett, the job is yours if you want it. I have to say though, I am curious. You've been a butler for thirty-odd years. You're about my age. How is it that you have already retired, moved to New York, and are installed in a suite at the Carlyle? Are you loaded, or what?"

At that, Bennett roared with laughter.

"My son is a private banker, Madame. He has advised me on investments and he and I have done very well. He is a good son. I am proud of the way he turned out. He, too, plans to retire soon and begin a second career doing something to help world monuments. He and his family and I have traveled a good deal together and I think becoming an amateur archaeologist is an excellent plan for the next stage of his life. I believe entering your household will be an excellent plan for me. I find the suggested stipend agreeable and would like very much to view the cottage."

Shortly Bennett was installed. He likes it up here. He has his friends and I have mine and if the two occasionally overlap, so be it. I'll grant you our relationship is unconventional but, as Uncle Ralph said, a foolish consistency is the hobgoblin of little minds.

In the winter months, we arrange our schedule so that someone is always in the country in case of an extended power outage or some weather catastrophe.

If we are traveling together in winter, his daughter-in-law sometimes brings the children for sledding, or we have the housekeeper stay over.

I wouldn't exactly say that we are like a family---I am an only child and have a murky notion of family---but I will say we have reached a happy equilibrium and it is nice to come home to someone, some of the evenings, some of the time.

AUTOPSY

'Twas the morning before Christmas and all through the house, not a creature was stirring except those going to an autopsy.

Until the new county office building gives him his own quarters, our medical examiner performs his tasks in a suite of rooms next to the morgue in the basement of the local hospital. The hospital serves two counties, ours and the one across the river.

When I first moved here, the hospital was smallish but over the last two decades has tripled in size and I gather has similarly upgraded staff competencies. Thankfully, I've never had to find out first-hand. I parked in the front lot and carefully walked across icy moguls toward the lobby. After signing in at the desk, I went over to the elevators and noticed a plaque honoring Mrs. Oliver North. They're from Philmont, a wide spot in the road a few miles past Claverack. Two Indian doctors, a plump practical nurse with a rose tattooed on her forearm, and three Candy Stripers waited for the elevator with me.

The autopsy had been postponed until the examiner, Frank Carver---I would prefer you not ask about his name---had managed to make it back from a snow-bound Christmas trip to Rochester. Our town's famous poet, John Ashbery, is from outside Rochester and once paraphrased

Whitman, saying up there in the north country he "heard America snowing."

I rode down three floors and turned left down the fluorescent hallway, trying to ignore the antiseptic tang. I knocked on the door marked 'Examiner—Do Not Enter,' and entered an office with a Steelcase desk, a computer, printer and vertical files on a maple credenza behind the desk, one wall of bookshelves and another covered by a blackboard and a mirror, although with the overhead lighting in this place, who needs a mirror?

I called, "Hello?" and walked toward Paul's 'in here' through a slightly open door to find myself in the examining room facing Paul and the medical examiner.

The morgue floor and walls were white tiled. A nine-body refrigeration unit, three across, three deep, stood against the east wall. A stainless steel anatomic autopsy table stood in the center of the room, its sink at the left end, electric cables running across the floor to its base. An instrument table stood to one side, calipers, scissors, saws, and other instruments precisely arranged on a white towel. The other three walls were lined with cabinets, shelves, and drawers topped with steel counters on which sat microscopes, a small centrifuge, rows of test tubes, boxes of slides, and other forensic paraphernalia. Four black rubber aprons hung on wall hooks. A great triple sink stood in one corner. I felt the chill of the room.

Taking my elbow, Paul said, "Good morning, Lindsey. Thanks for coming. This is Frank Carver. Frank, Lindsey Brooks. Lindsey is auditing this course."

"Dr. Carver," I said. We shook hands and I found myself looking into the face of a man with a great shock of red hair gone deeply gray at the temples. His hands had red hair, his freckled forearms had red hair. He wore a lab coat open over a dark green sweater, a blue shirt, and a subdued green paisley tie.

"We've finished up here late last night. Sorry about the delay. Hell of a time getting out of Rochester. Do you wish to view the body?" Apparently Dr. Carver was addressing only me as Paul said nothing.

I said I did not. I have never seen a dead body other than a few heavily-rouged, meticulously groomed specimens in coffins and prefer to keep it that way.

"In that case," he said, picking up a file and a clipboard from a table, "let's go into the office." We filed out and the temperature warmed noticeably. I had skipped my morning cereal and my head began to swim slightly. I was relieved when he said, "If you will please sit down," gesturing to chairs, and striding briskly to the swivel chair behind the desk, "I will take you through the results of our examination."

Paul and I settled ourselves in two chocolate Naugahyde chairs facing Carver and the blackboard behind him.

"Five feet four inches. 105 pounds. According to the physician at the murder scene that night, death occurred between four and six o'clock.

"Neither hair nor blood nor internal organs revealed toxins or poisons, nor prescription or OTC drugs of any kind, nor alcohol. A very clean system."

Paul interrupted, "We weren't expecting poison, were we? The woman was hanged."

Mr. Carver answered, "There is very slight bruising on the neck, but not at all consistent with death by hanging."

"What?" Paul asked, frowning. "Everyone saw her at the end of a rope."

"Hanging was long-favored by the judiciary, Sheriff, and, as a result, we know quite a lot of specifics about that manner of dying. Hanging's mechanism of death is effectively decapitation, with traumatic spondylolysis---that is, crushing---of the second cervical vertebra, known as 'hangman fracture,' and transection, severing, of the spinal cord. Hanging's popularity with the courts lay in its efficiency. It's a snap, as it were."

Dr. Carver smiled.

I shuddered and thought I saw Paul do the same. Carver said, "I assure you an examination of her spinal cord rules out hanging."

Paul leaned forward. "Was she attacked? Was there a struggle?"

He shook his head. "Nothing to indicate such on the greater corpus. No head injuries. No bruises, contusions, no marks of any kind on her body."

"No bangs on the head? No bruising? How could that be? What about trace material under her nails?" Paul asked impatiently.

"If you will allow me to present the facts without incessant interruption, Sheriff, you may profit from our analysis." Carver paused. "I am also interested to see if you arrive at the same conclusion I have reached."

Paul pressed his lips together tightly.

"Sorry," he said. "Go ahead."

"Absent the criteria for hanging, we must work, therefore, on the assumption that she was dead before the rope was put around her neck. This leaves us with several possibilities to eliminate. Technically, my finding as written in the report is 'death by venous obstruction, leading to cerebral stagnation, hypoxia, and unconsciousness.' "

Shaking my head, I asked, "Forgive me, what is hypoxia?"

"Hypoxia occurs when the brain's supply of oxygen and glucose is interrupted. Even a relatively short interruption, mere moments, triggers a cascade of abnormal events, the fatal problem being cerebral ischemia."

Paul and I frowned.

"Remember your Greek?" Dr. Carver asked.

"Only Latin for me, sorry," I answered. Four years of it, but no Greek. Another reason to regret not having gone to Exeter.

Paul said, "My Greek is limited to feta."

Carver continued. "Ischemia. From the Greek *iskhaimos*, a stopping of the blood : *iskhein*, to keep back + *haima*, blood. A low-oxygen state caused by arterial obstruction or lack of blood supply. Any number of things can cause it --- suffocation, head trauma, carbon monoxide poisoning, cardiac arrest, strangling. It can even occur as a complication of general anesthesia.

"We had to consider each of these six possibilities in the death of Sheila Marks.

"First, and presumably least likely, was she under general anesthesia? No. Anesthesia leaves residue in the lungs, blood, and tissue which persists for up to six months. Her tissue samples reflect no such elements.

"Secondly, did she succumb to carbon monoxide poisoning? Again, the lungs would be implicated. We found no traces of carbon monoxide.

"Thirdly, head trauma. I have told you her skull bears no evidence of catastrophic head injury.

"Fourth, stroke. Though it is unlikely that a young woman---records show she was forty years of age---would suffer stroke, that possibility also had to be eliminated. I examined the brain for the subdural damage that would indicate a cerebral infarction. There is no evidence of stroke.

"Because the bruising around the throat is very slight, possibly caused merely by the weight of her body against the rope, I initially suspected suffocation--- in the strict medico-legal sense, obstruction of respiration by means other than direct pressure on the neck. Pillows usually come to mind. To ascertain evidence of suffocation, one dissects the neck after the great vessels of the thorax have been emptied, achieving scrutiny of the lungs in a relatively bloodless field. But her lungs afford none of the platelet congestion consistent with asphyxiation. We can therefore eliminate suffocation.

"This leaves us with strangulation.

"Depending on how the patient was strangled, we would expect to find abrasions, lacerations, contusions, edema to the neck, or Tardieu spots---clotting---at the site of choking. However, as I said a moment ago, there is only faint bruising on the neck. Ordinarily, in cases of manual strangulation, one finds disc-like finger-tip bruises. These, too, are absent.

"Assuming strangulation, we look for lateral finger-nail scratches on the neck, primarily self-inflicted as the victim struggles to remove the assailant's hands. These are also conspicuously absent on Ms Marks' body.

"Her neck has none of the deeper bruises left by fingers probing more brutally. We find no blueness of the tongue consistent with sustained, violent pressure---'throttling,' as it is known in England---no hemorrhage under the skin of the neck or bruising of the strap muscles. There is no damage to the larynx or crushing of the superior horns of the thyroid cartilage or the greater horns of the hyoid bone.

"Neither do we find evidence of any ligature. No marks left by a rope or wire.

"No, she was not hanged. She was definitely strangled. But very softly strangled."

Dr. Carver paused. Paul leaned forward and asked, "I find it impossible to understand why there are no bruises, no signs of a struggle. The woman was not one to go quietly. If she had been attacked, she must have put up a fight. How could there have been no marks of any kind on a naked body?"

"Simply because she was nude when the body was discovered does not mean she was naked when she was killed. We can conjecture that she was strangled when clothed, then undressed and suspended by the rope."

I asked, "You said she had been 'softly strangled.' How is it possible to kill someone gently?"

"Fairly easily," Dr. Carver said, and standing, walked over to stand directly in front of me. "Ms. Brooks, would you mind removing your scarf? And slip off your jacket. I'll illustrate what I mean."

I stood and untied the heavy scarf wrapped around my neck. Under my jacket I was wearing a v-neck sweater over a cotton shirt with some buttons undone, so exposing my neck and throat was an easy matter.

Dr. Carver took my jacket and hung it over the back of a chair. Then he repositioned me slightly so that I faced Paul and the mirror on the wall behind him. Paul looked uncomfortable and I felt cold again.

The doctor brushed aside my hair and spread the collar of my blouse. "Here," he said, lightly grasping the front of my throat with his right hand. His fingertips were smooth and cool against my skin.

"You're an athlete, aren't you? Nicely developed musculature approaching the neck. Even so, it remains vulnerable, easily the most vulnerable point of the body."

He placed his index finger into the hollow at the base of my throat.

"No bones to shield this area. No protection of any kind, just a strip of skin. And behind that? Clusters of important things. Less than a half inch away we have the windpipe and a clear path to the spinal cord.

"But in strangulation, the greater risk lies here," and he used both hands to trace lines from below my ears down either side of my neck.

"Of all the blood vessels in one's body, the veins and arteries within the neck are uniquely vulnerable to compression injuries. First, the veins. We have two jugular veins on each side, here and here, one almost at the surface, one running barely a centimeter below. Both are critical to maintaining blood pressure. When jugular blood flow is disrupted, even slightly, the heart must instantly compensate---but, alas, it cannot. And we have congestive heart failure.

"And now, the arteries. The carotids, very large vessels, are here," and his fingers moved up, then down on my neck, "one on either side, branching directly off the aorta. These are the main arteries to the brain. Turning again to our Greek friends, we learn 'karotides' relates to the words *katotikos,* stupefying, and *karos,* deep sleep. The ancients knew firm pressure on the carotid arteries renders a person unconscious. 'Karotides' also led to the Spanish word 'garrote', both a method and implement of strangulation. Garroting"--- here Carver whipped clenched fists across and together in front of him to illustrate--- "causes not only 'deep sleep,' insensibility, but often, 'permanent sleep'--- death.

"These vessels offer an extremely expedient route to death. Compared to blood vessels, the airway and the spinal column play minimal roles in the immediate death of strangulation victims.

"In Sheila Marks' death, as in every strangulation, the brain suc-cumbs---and very, very quickly. These are my findings."

Paul's eyes met mine. Softly strangled.

"I haven't had time to make a copy of this," he said to Paul, handing him the file. "But you'll find a Xerox machine down the hall."

Paul took the file and walked out the door

"I don't suppose you're in the mood for coffee?" Dr. Carver asked, shifting his glasses up to the top of his head. He removed his lab coat and held my jacket for me. Sitting on the edge of the desk, he unfolded his cuffs, and began rebuttoning them.

"Perhaps another time," I demurred. "I'm afraid all of this has been unsettling. I think I'd better be alone with my thoughts."

"Ah yes," he said, hanging up his lab coat and putting on a suede jacket.

"I understand. Perhaps another time. I hope you won't confuse me with the grim reaper, Ms. Brooks. I'm not. I'm just assisting with his memoirs."

A VISIT TO THE POST ROAD INN

After leaving Dr. Carver, Paul and I drove up to the Post Road Inn to check out Ted Marks' alibi, me with my window down to clear the hospital smell from my nose and lungs.

We parked in a gravel lot in front of a ramshackle, shingled building with neon beer signs in the windows. Inside, the requisite pool table stood in one corner. A darts board hung on one wall beside a few pinball machines. A genuine rarity, a shuffleboard table, stood in the middle of the room. Chairs rested upside down on the tabletops. The bar ran along the left side of the room. Honky-tonks may be lively places during the evenings, but they are seedy in daylight.

A teenager with a green Mohawk and fatigue pants was mopping the floor. A man sat behind the counter in the corner, smoking a cigarette, working on a calculator, and writing notes in a ledger.

As we walked in he said, "Sorry, folks. We're not open. Come back at noon."

We continued walking toward him, winding between tables and upturned chair legs, nonchalantly slipping off our coats and tossing them on the bar. We sat down on stools directly in front of the barkeep who said, "I'm sure you got it bad to be in here at this time of day, but I really can't help you for another hour. Law says we can't pull a tap until noon."

Turning to me, Paul echoed, "Man says we're too early. Shoot! Take care of that for me, would you, Sweetikins."

I don't know where he gets these names. I raised my left arm, pushed up my sleeve and reset my watch to noon, holding it out so both men could see.

"Time do fly when you're thirsty," Paul observed.

"How's about two short drafts? Those little glasses over there'll be just fine. Not the Genny, the Bud Light."

The bartender grinned and drew two beers.

"I like your style," he said, placing two glasses in front of us. "Just don't let the sheriff catch you coercing me like that. Cheers."

"This your place?" Paul asked.

"Yeah, for almost ten years now. You never been here before?"

"No, but you keep being hospitable and we'll be regulars," I smiled. "In fact, it was one of your regulars who suggested we drop by."

"Who's that?"

"Ted Marks. You know him?"

"Teddy! What a great guy! Hell of a thing about his wife. He was sitting right there on that chair the night it happened."

"No kidding?"

"Nobody wants to miss our Christmas party! Prizes for best Santa, best Mrs. Santa, and best elf costumes. Also shuffleboard, darts, and pool contests. Ted came in after work about four and was playing three guys from the Thruway Authority in shuffleboard. He'd have won, too, if he hadn't already claimed victory in his beer and bourbon shots sprint. He got pretty woozy and had to have a little lie-down."

"Where would a person have a little lie-down?"

"Right here in my private office." He turned, slipped off the stool, and opened the door behind him to reveal a shabby but tidy office with a scarred wooden desk, two worn kitchen chairs and a sofa that sang out Salvation Army. The one window looked out on a fenced field and a handful of cows munching through the snow.

"Were you bartending all evening?" Paul asked.

The barkeep nodded.

"And Ted was here all night? How would you know if he had left? Pretty busy tending bar for Santa and those elves, wasn't it?"

The bartender folded his arms across his chest.

"You a cop?"

"I'm the sheriff."

"This about the murder?"

Paul nodded.

"I can guarantee Ted Marks was here all evening. You can ask anybody. He was three sheets to the wind when I put him on the couch in here. Must've been close to six then. You think he went out the window? Yeah, he could have gone out but he wouldn't have got too far. My wife had his car."

"Why was that?" I asked.

"Me and Ted and Lucy, my wife, all went to high school together. That's how long I've known him. My wife's mother is in the home over to Chatham and my wife wanted to go see her. Ted told her to take his car as he wasn't going anywhere in his condition."

"You don't have a car?" Paul looked skeptical.

Who better to lie than an old high school buddy?

"My wife's is in the shop and the kids had mine gone to the mall in Kingston. You know kids and shopping. After he snoozed for a couple of hours, old Ted bounced back. The party was in high gear and he led the crowd singing carols during the darts throwing. He stayed until almost midnight. Incidentally, you're not the first people checking up on him about that night."

"No kidding? Who would that have been?"

61

"Some big, good-lookin' blonde gal that worked for his wife."

At that, Paul and I hopped off our stools. Paul reached in his pocket to pay but the barkeep waved him off.

"Told you. Can't sell beer until noon. "

When we got back into town it was time for lunch. We called Olana to make sure Eve was in, then went to Cascades on Warren Street where the soups are homemade and delicious. People who grew up here remember when Cascades was the old Greek's soda fountain before the movie theatre next door burned down. The couple who bought it in 1990 have made a real go of it. The courthouse and police station are right around the corner so the place is packed with lawyers and officers during the week and today was no exception. We ate quickly and kept our voices down as we discussed our visit to the Post Road Inn.

Paul said, "So Marks' alibi holds, more or less. I suppose he could have gone out the window, hitchhiked to Olana, killed his wife, and then hitchhiked back in time for the darts final. But given when the bartender said he passed out and what Carver said about time of Sheila's death, the timing would have been tricky."

I nodded. "It's easy to fake being drunk. But hard to fake drinking when someone else is pouring the shots and watching you down them. Also, who wakes up from a drunken stupor and suddenly decides to climb out a window and hitchhike twenty miles on a frigid night to kill his wife? I doubt it. The question is why would Eve have been checking up on his alibi?"

"Wanted to know if he killed her boss?"

"We've got one too many amateur sleuths here. Let's go. I've thought of a few other questions for Eve anyway."

We went in the back door of Olana to find Eve at her desk. I noticed that while she had looked schoolmarmish a few days ago, today she looked very snappy in a dark blue wool suit and good heels.

"Hello, Eve. Thanks for seeing us." Paul said.

Eve said, "Before we start, you wanted the key to Sheila's desk. I have it."

We all trooped down the hall and went into Sheila's office where Eve unlocked the lower drawer of Sheila's desk. At the bottom lay a Hudson High School annual from 1954.

Paul picked up the book and flipped through it. "This is several years before me," he said. "Maybe her parents' class? Sentimentality, I guess?" He put the book back in the drawer.

As we headed to her office, Eve said, "What's on your mind today, Sheriff?"

"A few follow-up questions. Go ahead, Lindsey."

"I'm just curious about how this place is managed, Eve. Do all of the employees report to you?"

"Basically, yes, except the curatorial staff, of course. That's Van der Wyck's bailiwick."

"You seem like a person who would run a tight ship."

With a modest smile she said, "I try."

"You've been promoted over the years? Have you been given raises?"

"A few. But this is not the place to work if you plan on getting rich."

"I don't believe Sheila actually had a management degree, did she?"

"No, but after she became director, she went to several Harvard seminars on managing not-for-profits. There's no question this place needed a higher level of professionalism. She put new procedures in place, mostly having to do with accountability. We all had to write down goals and plans for the year. I reviewed these with my staff twice each year to check on progress and make course corrections."

"And you met with Sheila to see how you were doing?"

She nodded. "Same thing. I wrote a plan and we met twice a year so she could evaluate my work. Of course, if there was something she wanted me or anyone else on the staff to do, she let us know right away."

Paul said, "I'd like to see everyone's evaluations."

"I don't see why that's necessary." She bristled.

Paul spoke up. "Eve, we are trying to determine why the woman was killed. There might be a motive in those reviews. A disgruntled employee, maybe. Or someone with a grudge."

She unlocked a filing cabinet and pulled out a thick folder of papers.

"These are from the past year," she said, handing the folder to Paul. "We have them going back for about six years."

Paul took half and handed me the rest. We scanned in silence for several minutes. Since most of the people reported to Eve, most notes and comments were hers. Sheila's initials were on very short paragraphs appended to Eve's evaluations. Her remarks sounded like a martinet. 'Dirty uniform. Late to staff meeting. Not a team player. Cluttered office.' From time to time I glanced up at Eve who was fiddling with things on her desk or staring at her hands and frowning.

I looked up from my reading and said, "Says here Manny Feller was due to be replaced. Why was that?"

Eve frowned.

"Sheila felt he was too old. She wanted to get a professional landscaper to manage the grounds. Manny's old enough to retire but I doubt he wants to. He's still strong as a horse and he's a hard worker. I never have to tell him what to do, he just knows."

"Your review is pretty unflattering," Paul observed.

"Says you are uncomfortable with authority. Impatient. Too familiar with people who report to you. Too forward with board members. Sounds like Sheila felt you were overstepping your boundaries."

Eve tossed her head and said sharply, "Listen, I know what I do here is valuable. She'd have had a time replacing me, but I wasn't after her job. Sheila was never satisfied with anyone, whether it was someone who worked for her, or…." She stopped abruptly.

"Or what?" Paul asked.

"Or someone who was married to her?" I suggested.

Eve nodded slowly. "That's right. Or someone who was married to her."

"What did you know about her marriage?"

"I knew she got a great guy but she couldn't care less."

"Why did you go to the Post Road Inn to check up on Ted's alibi?" I asked.

"I wanted to know if Ted was there. I couldn't believe he would have…"

"Killed her? Did you think he wanted to?"

"Of course he didn't kill her. But he detested her and wanted to leave her. He just couldn't bring himself to admit the marriage was finished and make a new life. God knows I gave him every opportunity to."

HUXLEY'S PARTY

Because of what I would refer to as a dicey childhood, Christmas has always been fraught, if not with terror, then a lot of free-floating angst. Plus which having a corpse up the hill was not my idea of revelry.

Plus Bennett was in town for Christmas with his son.

Fortunately, I had Huxley's Christmas Eve party.

Huxley Smythe is an old and dear friend and the doyen of the Hudson Valley 400. He lives in an 18th century Beekman manor house that is decorated in a cross between Vaux le Vicomte and Billy Baldwin. Huxley wrote sparkling comedies and dramas during television's Golden Age. He now writes plays and his memoirs, a constant worry to any of us who have misbehaved in his presence which includes every soul I know. Hux dissects other individuals when speaking to me and I can only assume that I am similarly flayed when other ears are present.

Wise, arch, and unflappable, Huxley throws legendary parties---his Christmas Eve fête is a glorious antidote for the demoralization of the season. It features friends greeting friends, enemies greeting enemies, and an immense Transylvanian ham.

Forty cars lined the driveway beneath the pines when I arrived. The house blazed with lights and I could hear the party the moment I opened the car door and stepped out, watching for icy patches. *Not* wearing the Valentino, you'll be relieved to hear.

Huxley's affectionate pug, Achilles, performed welcoming arabesques as I dropped my overnight bag in the foyer and headed off toward the pantry in search of my host and a tumbler of vodka.

Evergreen swags lay across every mantle and above the doors, their crisp smell mingling with the fragrances of the revelers cavorting amid Huxley's gorgeous rugs and beautiful, bold furnishings. A twelve foot Christmas tree stood in the front hall, steadied by guy wires attached to the banister.

I moved through the animated mob, good-looking in bright reds, black velvets, plaid jackets, lots of extravagant stoles, and good jewelry.

Huxley is always notoriously short-handed in the help department and so we regulars are pressed into service to supplement the staff.

"Thank God, you're here!" my host exclaimed as I joined him in the pantry, he resplendent in a purple brocade smoking jacket.

"Open these!" he said, gesturing to a flock of bottles. He thrust a corkscrew into my hand and gave me a big kiss. I obediently started in on my task as he poured me a glass of Gray Goose and began arranging wine glasses on a chinoiserie tray.

"Terribly attractive crowd this year," I shouted above the din. "I saw Nadia nuzzling with Graham, presumably happy with her settlement. And is Helen here *with* Frank? When did that start up again?"

"My dear," he crooned, "I predict grave outcomes for many tonight. Veronica, as you know, is involved in at least three triangles swirling around her this evening. It cannot end well. I just hope they don't break anything--of mine.

"Then we have Bertram, Bagwell, and Bobby who any *second* will discover that they have shared much, much more than a dementia for Directoire furniture.

"And, not two minutes ago, Francine was overheard to screech at Fernanda, 'You *burned* my letters??!!??!' Those two ladies are now on the back porch and I fear for the wicker.

"*No, Consuelo, no!*" Huxley gestured frantically to his housekeeper who was steaming toward the dining room with a tower of Fiesta ware. "Not the breakfast china! The bittersweet, Consuelo! *Nighttime plates!*"

My host sighed as he filled goblets with a Sicilian red.

"I assume you are going to divulge every detail you have learned about the dead nude at Olana. You must or I will withhold your eggnog and your Christmas stocking."

"Oh, Huxley," I demurred. "Not on Christmas Eve. Let's make merry tonight and save the felonies for Christmas morning before presents. We'll get down to brass tacks over coffee and our lumps of coal."

"Well, my dear, you may not be able to put it off. One of your chief suspects is standing right over there." As we moved into the study, Huxley gestured to a man standing against the mantle.

It was the same tall and elegant man I had seen at Olana, with silver hair and beard.

"Every inch the squire," I observed. "I noticed him at Olana before all hell broke loose. Why should I suspect him of hoisting poor Sheila? Tell me about him."

"Lucius Wrangel, the Russian émigré and financier par excellence. I'll introduce you. I knew him slightly years ago when he invested in one of my plays."

"Ah, yes. The mystery donor. A handsome specimen. Looks very fit," I opined.

"Oh, yes," said Huxley. "Marvelous diet. He eats people alive.

"Lucius!" he exclaimed. "Allow me to present one of my more successful protégés, Lindsey Brooks."

We shook hands. "Your reputation has preceded you, Ms. Brooks."

"Welcome to the Valley, Mr. Wrangel," I said. "Huxley tells me you've acquired a parcel nearby on Carnegie Lane."

He looked startled. "A parcel? I don't think you'd call five hundred acres a 'parcel'."

"Ahhh, that's just my vaunted gift of understatement," I smiled. "Tell me about the palatial manse."

He beamed. "It's one of the old Delano estates. This one came into my hands when the previous owner's checkbook cracked under the strain of restoration. He was a former business associate of mine and I was glad to be there at the right time. I still have the place on Fifth Avenue, of course, but at this point in my life, I enjoy the country more and more."

"How would you describe the earlier phase?" I asked.

He laughed and clinked his glass against mine. "Let's just say I was a wheeler dealer. Downtown was very good to me and now I'm here to join all you delightful people who want to protect and preserve this lovely part of the country."

"Well, God knows there are enough old houses and enough good causes to get involved in. Where will you begin your philanthropy?"

This was definitely the right tack to take. Lucius brightened considerably, spread his arms and exclaimed, "Exactly! First, I am giving a new Church painting to Olana."

"Yes, I saw it at the party. I'm afraid you were rather robbed of the limelight."

His face darkened. "One of the most terrible things I have ever seen. A tragedy. She was a bright young woman with a great future. True, she had her detractors—but, my God, look at what the woman had accomplished! It's Olana's loss. I saw you there that night, but I was in such a state of shock I was speechless."

"Please tell me about the portrait," I asked, if only to change the subject. "Where could you possibly have found a new Church? It's extraordinary!"

"On my very first trip, I was doing what every visitor to Hudson does---browsing the antique stores on Warren Street, popping in and out, seeing what was there. And I found it in Attique! You know that wonderful store at the top of Warren Street?"

I nodded.

"I bought a painting, a primitive Mexican landscape, and in having it restored, found the Church behind it. Damned lucky. Imagine discovering an unknown Church a stone's throw from the man's house! Astonishing!"

Others began to vie for Wrangel's attention. He and I had only one other exchange---his suggestion that I see him in the city for lunch, my suggestion that he come to me for dinner the first week in January.

Breakfast with Huxley

The next morning, as we sat in our pajamas and robes by a wonderful, warm fire in his study, coffee in hand, I debriefed Huxley, telling him what we knew so far.

When I had finished rehearsing the details, I asked, "What's your take on the characters?"

Huxley sighed and shook his head.

"My dear, you are walking through a veritable forest of motives," he said, setting down his mug and taking the pug into his lap.

"Martha Lee, as you well know, as everyone knows, is an unstable specimen. One can only guess at the number of her neuroses or the magnitude of her paranoia."

"Aren't you exaggerating slightly?" I laughed.

"Don't be naïve. This is a woman whose former husband filed for divorce on grounds of assault. This is a woman who has been in the best sanitariums for God-knows-what three times that I'm aware of. She has a house account at Silver Hill. When her father died, she went into complete decline and has since searched daily for a god-like figure to take his place.

"Lindsey, you have a Pollyannaish tendency to view every eccentric as quaintly annoying but harmless. I would suggest that Martha is a very willful child with a lot of barely suppressed anger who is becoming a rather desperate figure. Appearances to the contrary, she's that unfortunate species, the closet case. She's not getting any younger and she may have seen Lucius as the last, best chance to verify her status, not only as an attractive, desirable heterosexual, but as the Great Man's Wife, the sun in the Valley around which all planets must orbit. You know how people from Virginia are. Warped to the core.

"Finally, she's being railroaded out of the inner circle at Olana, supplanted by a classic arriviste. I don't think you can discount her."

Huxley frowned and I could see he was serious.

"What about van der Wyck?"

"A man whose professional pride is on the line. Biggest fish in a small pond until the blonde comes along. Shunted aside, left at his dreary desk to scribble monographs about the role of embroidery scissors in Olana's window traceries while the babe is at the Rainbow Room or Bouley's or Michael's, hobbing my dear, nobbing my dear. Must have driven him right over the edge. You know nothing is angrier than an academic who's been passed over. *And* he's a fitness nut---spends *days* lifting weights, darling. I'm sure he'd show his abs to anyone who asked nicely. He would have had no trouble strangling the woman---and very few qualms.

"As for her assistant, she's after the spotlight, the job, and the husband. The bitter, unappreciated understudy, seething with ambition, waiting for her moment to take center stage. To speed her career along, she devised an early exit for the star.

"Then we have the poor drunken husband. The football hero gone wrong, the barrister who left his career in a bar room. He still carries a torch, she's his only shot at redemption, he cannot bear abandonment. He planned to kill himself, too, but lost his nerve, or could only locate one rope. Another sordid possibility to sort out. It'll be a great part for Robert Downey in the movie. I think I smell the bacon."

While Huxley was in the kitchen, I called and left a message for Paul. We needed to talk to Ted Marks again.

Huxley returned with plates of scrambled eggs and oven-baked prosciutto.

74

"The biggest fish will be the most difficult to catch," he observed.

"You can't mean Wrangel? Why is he a suspect at all?"

"Partly because he is the most powerful player in the cast of characters. How can you discount him?"

"Because he had nothing to gain from Sheila's death. How long have you known him? How did you meet?"

"My lamented late wife, Helène, went through a Russian icon phase and Lucius is an expert. She really only liked the icons for the gold, of course, but she didn't tell him that. She considered them more ornamental than Audubons and a better investment than another Matisse drawing.

"There was an exhibit at La Vielle Russie. Helène was in a very hot Broadway show at the time and had just won a Tony. Lucius singled us out and walked us through the exhibit, explaining the finer points of Russian iconography. Afterwards, he took us to dinner and was perfectly charming. He spoke very movingly about his family's horrific experiences in St. Petersburg during the war. But I thought there was something disingenuous about him, as though his every word had been carefully scripted and delivered many times before to different audiences in different rooms. But, of course, I'm sure it had—and nothing wrong with that.

"I can't put my finger on it. He's here in a few days for dinner. You'll come. And bring that adorable butler!"

After instantly agreeing, I left Huxley to his domain, his memoirs, Achilles' dog hair, and his grandchildren who were screaming for him as they streaked in the back door.

Bennett returned home in the afternoon and we settled in around our own Christmas tree.

A VISIT TO DR. WISHMAN

Paul and I took the train down to the city to follow up on the doctor's appointment in Sheila Mark's calendar.

Because he doesn't make the trip as often as I do, I gave Paul the window seat for one of the world's great train rides, right up there with the Geneva to Como route or the trip through the Rockies.

The Hudson River originates at Lake Tear-of-the-Clouds in the wildest part of the Adirondack Mountains in northeastern New York. From an elevation of 4,322 feet, this small mountain stream flows south, dropping some 60 feet per mile in the upper regions.

The Hudson has many contributing streams and tributaries, the largest being the Indian, Schroon, and Sacondaga Rivers and many beautiful falls and rapids between the Adirondacks and Troy which are used as power sources, supporting many types of mills over the years. Just above Troy, several large tributaries join the Hudson, the Batten Kill, Fish Creek, the Hoosic River, and the mighty Mohawk.

From Troy to the mouth of the river in New York harbor, the Hudson River is at sea level, therefore tidal and an estuary. Although the Hudson has a total length of only about 315 miles---the longest river, the Nile, is 4,100 miles and the Mississippi almost 2,400---it has been one of the most significant factors in the development of the United States. Navigable for almost 150 miles inland, it invited early exploration. In 1524, Verrazano investigated the river for a short distance, but it was Henry Hudson who explored its extent, sailing up to the mouth of the Mohawk near Albany in 1609. In the eighteenth century, during the American Revolution, control of the River determined control of the country and one-third of the colonists' battles against the British were fought on its shores. The Battle of Saratoga was arguably the most important of the war as it finally ended British hopes of controlling the River.

The opening of the Erie Canal in the nineteenth century, connecting the River not only with western New York but with the western United States beyond, insured New York City's emergence as the premiere metropolis in the new world.

The nineteenth century also produced Robert Fulton's *Clermont,* the first steamship. This transportation breakthrough allowed cities to grow along the River and trade to flourish, increased population and tourism in the Valley, and encouraged the great estates along the Hudson that made the area, it is said, America's own Loire Valley.

Aside from spectacular scenery, the trip is a virtual history book of Valley lore. Each lighthouse along the way has its own architectural style---the one at Saugerties even receives overnight guests. At Staatsburg, the train dips underground into a private tunnel built in the 1850s by an imperious estate owner who didn't want to see or hear the Iron Horse. Edgewater, formerly Gore Vidal's delightful neo-classical house, now in the illustrious Jenrette collection, is so close to the tracks the Meissen shivers when the Wolverine roars by. Halfway to New York, the ruins of Bannerman's Castle stand as a reminder of the perils of hoarding explosives.

Just south of Poughkeepsie, we passed the Harriman Bridge, a classic example of progress fueled by opportunism. The fascinating little tale began in 1910 when Averill Harriman's father and some friends donated land for the Bear Mountain State Park and got a whopping tax write-off. The Park, which also boasts a leg of the Appalachian Trail, was so popular and generated so much traffic a bridge was needed to cross the Hudson. Smelling more money, Harriman and partners formed a company and built one. When completed in 1924, the Bear Mountain Bridge was the longest suspension bridge in the world. Its innovative cable construction pioneered a golden age of long-span building, making possible such goliaths as the George Washington and the Golden Gate.

Bear Mountain Bridge opened as a private entity in 1924, charging eighty cents a car. That is the equivalent of $9 today, more than any other bridge or tunnel in the United States. Harriman et al operated it for thirty years, making almost $75 million, then sold it to New York State for not quite $25 million, all in today's money. Those clever Harrimans.

Moments later we passed through Sing Sing prison which straddles the tracks, causing Paul to reminisce happily about felons who had been put away during his tenure in New York City and how he hoped to have the opportunity to do the same with Sheila's murderer. Thanks to several memorable films noir, Sing Sing lives in the consciousness of anyone over fifty as the origin of the phrase 'send up the river' and the home of the Electric Chair. Named after the Sint Sinck Indians, the prison sits on the site of the 18th century Silver Mine Farm where silver, gold, and copper had been found.

The site also offered a rich marble quarry. In May 1825, the first hundred convicts arrived by barge from the Erie Canal and began cutting stone to build their prison. As the quarrying expanded, the prison provided stone for Renwick's Grace Church on Broadway, New York University, and City Hall in Albany. Thanks to enterprising wardens over the years, Sing Sing's highly profitable contract labor---no wages, you see---was provided to an ever-widening variety of industries, including making boots, shoes, hats, brushes, mattresses, and hogsheads for rum dealers.

The Electric Chair made its debut at Sing Sing in 1890. Over time, the invention dispatched, among some six hundred or so others, the Rosenbergs, Sacco and Vanzetti and Willie Sutton, the famed heist artist, who explained he robbed banks 'because that's where the money is.'

During the Twenties, the New York Yankees played exhibition games against Sing Sing inmates and other teams. In 1925, when the

Yankees played the New York Giants, Babe Ruth blasted his longest home run 620 feet over the right field wall.

Ten minutes from New York, the George Washington Bridge hove into sight as we passed the Palisades, which rise sharply several hundred feet above the west bank of the River. The Palisades' impressive cliffs are two million year-old lava from the Triassic period. Thanks once again to the apparently boundless generosity of the Rockefeller family, we can admire this striking natural phenomenon preserved as an 80,000-acre park.

The pleasantness of the ride evaporated as we entered Pennsylvania Station, or rather, the ground floor of Madison Square Garden, as dreary a public space as anyone could imagine and a reason to wish Mrs. Onassis had achieved prominence years earlier. Jackie could surely have galvanized public opinion to save the old Penn Station just as she saved the grandest and most central of our terminals when it was threatened.

Outside we handed ten dollars to two homeless people, hailed a cab and headed up town, seeing throngs rushing toward Macy's for after-Christmas sales, through the garment district and its racks of frocks being wheeled through icy puddles, on to the lovely sight of carriages rolling slowly through a snowy Central Park, and shortly arriving around the corner from the Met at Eighty-sixth Street between Madison and Fifth.

Dr. Wishman's office was in a superb Beaux-Arts brownstone with a second story rounded oriel. My first thought was that a little girl from Hudson was seeing a very tony doctor.

Even though we had an appointment, the nurse coolly said we would have to wait. Paul read the sports section of the *Times* while I looked through a Sotheby's international real estate catalogue. Must ask Bennett to arrange a trip to Morocco---it looks stunning and everyone has been there except me.

After twenty minutes, Paul swore, threw the paper down, and went over to the nurse's desk. He said, "I sure want to thank you for your time. Please tell the doctor we were here and we are sorry we couldn't see him."

Nurse Olga smiled piteously. "I will tell the doctor. Good bye."

"Oh, and tell him when he gets the subpoena, be sure to ask for me by name at courthouse. Here's my card. Bye-bye."

This brought the witch to her feet. "Wait here!" she barked.

She returned instantly with a sharp-featured man in a white doctor's coat accessorized with a tangerine Hermes tie, charcoal pinstripe flannel trousers, and a fat Mont Blanc in his breast pocket. Central casting.

"I'm terribly sorry you had to wait," he murmured. "An emergency patient. Please come into my office."

He might as well have said, "Come into my deeply paneled and richly appointed office." Paul and I sat down beside a magnificent George III partners' desk while Dr. Wishman settled himself in a black leather wing chair opposite us. A Mensa certificate hung on the wall beside his academic degrees and medical accreditations. Built-in bookcases held hundreds of volumes on everything from the Krebs cycle to coffee table books on Greek and Roman antiquities. I could feel his eyes appraising us with barely contained distain. I wished Paul had not worn work boots or a Carhardt jacket over his sport coat. I was glad we were not interviewing with a co-op board or The Century membership committee. I fear Dr. Wishman had decided we were country bumpkins.

He leaned forward solicitously. "How can I help you?"

"You had an appointment scheduled for today with Sheila Marks."

"Yes, yes, of course. The death upstate. Appalling. Ms. Marks was a new patient. I really knew nothing about her so I'm afraid I can't be of much help."

"Lots of doctors in NYC. How'd she get to you?"

"As I recall, she was a referral."

"From whom?"

"I really don't recall."

"Why was she seeing you?"

"Naturally, I cannot reveal anything about the specific nature of my patient's…"

"Oh, can the confidentiality crap," Paul snapped.

"You're a ladies' doctor. Which means she had some lady issue. So, what? Lumps? Funny tubes? Wrong baby?"

Wishman stood and shoved his hands into his pockets.

"I'm not going to be spoken to like that by some yokel. Furthermore, I don't know where you get your information, but I am not…"

Paul interrupted before he could finish.

"Right. You're a doctor but your patient is dead and you don't want to talk to me because I'm a yokel. The easiest thing to do is give you a bigger venue. We'll toddle on back upstate. You sit here and wait until the order comes for your appearance in the Hudson courthouse. Take the train. The ride is lovely, you'll enjoy it."

I spoke up. "Wait! What were you saying? You're not…what?"

Wishman raised his hands and said loudly, "I am not a ladies' doctor! I don't do Ob-Gyn! I'm a plastic surgeon. A former patient and old friend, Lucius Wrangel, referred Sheila Marks to me. I never even met the woman. I did some work on Lucius a few years back and he recommended me."

"You never met Sheila Marks?"

He shook his head. "Absolutely not! We had one telephone conversation. She told me she wanted breast augmentation. She wanted me to give her bigger tits! We made an appointment for an examination."

Wishman nervously ran his hand through his hair.

"Look, you can understand my position. I have absolutely no connection to the woman! And I certainly don't want my name in the papers in connection with a murder. People jump to conclusions. You can imagine the effect it would have on my practice."

Paul and I left and walked up Fifth Avenue two blocks, turned on Eighty-sixth and went into the Neue Museum where I can always get a table, a professional courtesy extended after my help in recovering a Beckman which had gone astray en route from Berlin. We sat in the farthest corner booth and both ordered the wurst, the 'wienie lunch.'

"An unpleasant man," Paul remarked, looking glum after jumping the gun with Wishman.

"Bring me up to date on what you got at the house," I said. "Clues? Fingerprints? Murder weapon? Things left behind?"

"Nothing whatsoever. We've got a bunch of dead ends. I'm thinking we need a new angle. What I'd like to do is what we discussed on the train."

"Make a surprise visit to Lucius Wrangel?" I asked.

"Exactly."

A VISIT TO LUCIUS WRANGEL

Wrangel's office is in the old GM building, across from the Plaza Hotel. As we got out of our cab and walked past Grand Army Plaza, I was happy to see that the gilt on the Sherman statue was wearing off in several places.

We were crossing the building's promenade when Paul muttered one of his malaprops.

"You know, I've got a fifth sense about this Wrangel guy."

My eyes widened. I asked, "Really? Is it smell? Is it sight?"

Oblivious to my jibe, Paul continued, "New guy on the block. Eager to make a splash with the local set. Comes on strong with money. Poor little Sheila is infatuated. She decides she wants to become Mrs. Wrangel. He had to off her. Many a girl who sets her sights on a yacht winds up rowing her own boat."

I was about to point out that rowing a boat was a damned sight better than swinging from a noose, however I contented myself with pointing out the fallacy of his argument.

"Paul. Can't be. He's a gorgeous specimen but the guy's got to be hitting seventy. Not exactly prime time for a Casanova. Plus which, he only dates the glitterati---movie people, models. He's constantly in the Style Section or the social rags attending some gala accompanied by what I believe is called 'arm candy.' I hardly think Sheila was his type. If she had become infatuated, he'd just give her the brush, not kill her."

Wrangel's receptionist had been separated at birth from Dr. Wishman's receptionist. Another chilly, frightfully unattractive woman who informed us Mr. Wrangel was in a conference all day and was not to be disturbed. She was not enthused to hear 'Tell him the Sheriff wants to talk to him.' After the 'May I see some identification?' routine, Paul and I sat down to wait.

"I told you to wear your badge, Paul," I whispered. "People think the Sheriff thing is a ruse. They suspect you're selling exterminating services or toner for the copier. What's your approach going to be with Wrangel?"

"Oh, hell. I can handle Lucius Wrangel. I plan to find out what he knows and when he knew I knew it."

While we waited, I walked around looking at the curious collection of furniture assembled in the foyer. Paul and I were seated in a pair of Corbusier chairs. A table against the opposite wall was a French art nouveau bronze with marble inlay. A Werkstatte floor lamp stood between that and a Louis XV commode. All in all, I counted twelve design periods, none of which had ever been in the same room before.

I was trying to figure out what sort of sensibility would collect these things---was he just warehousing assets?---when the receptionist stood and said, "Mr. Wrangel will see you now. Briefly!" she warned with a smile worthy of Uta Hagen. Gratuitous again?

She led us toward two immense Jacobean doors that swung open automatically at our approach and closed behind her as she retired, leaving us alone in a deeply carpeted anteroom.

On our left, floor to ceiling glass afforded a magnificent view of Central Park. At that moment a mirrored panel to our right swiveled and Lucius Wrangel appeared.

Wrangel wore a light gray silk suit. Lobb slip-ons. Purple faille tie.

"Lindsey," he smiled and kissed me on the cheek. "What a pleasant surprise. Have you been deputized? Sheriff, good morning," he smiled, shaking hands with Paul.

I laughed. "I was in town anyway to look at some engravings and Sheriff Whitbeck promised me lunch if I'd keep him company. What a marvelous space! Breathtaking."

"My office is just through here," he said. The mirror swiveled again and we entered his office. A ten foot square glass table served as a desk. The walls held an extraordinary collection of paintings.

He had a dozen Russian avant garde pieces, including four Maleviches. There were also examples of primitivism, early cubism, and several of the abstracts called by the artists themselves, 'pointless exercises.' These faced six canvasses of the Bridge Group, riots of color. Behind his desk hung a single exceptional Bonnard. That was flanked by photos of Wrangel with presidents, mayors, artists, and framed citations for good works by major New York cultural institutions.

Paul walked over to the photographs and said, "Wow, you know a lot of big shots!"

"A lifetime of collecting?" I asked, gesturing to the art.

"My childhood was spent among beautiful things. Several of these pieces here were my parents'. They saw the new work in the early 20th century in Moscow and bought what they liked. I suppose you could say my parents were patrons."

I said, "I remember meeting you very casually years ago at a reception. I'm surprised and sorry our paths haven't crossed more frequently. You're clearly having a fascinating life. Art, business success, the social scene."

Paul asked, "Tell me, when did you leave Russia?"

"I was a little child. My parents and I were among the lucky few who escaped during the siege of St. Petersburg. Two years after the siege began, we fled the city across Lake Ladoga via the 'Road of Life'--- *Doroga Zhizni,*' he translated --- "the only route that connected the city with the mainland. During the warm season people were ferried across, and in winter, driven in trucks across the frozen lake. The route was under constant bombardment. We made it; many others did not.

"My parents and I made our way to Kotka, then to Helsinki. These paintings"---he gestured to the wall opposite the Park---"were the only possessions we saved, tightly rolled and hidden in the false tops and bottoms of luggage. Some silver and gold pieces, what remained of my mother's jewelry, and my own small coin collection were sewn into our coats. Those we used to pay our way. We traveled at night, moving across Finland, then Sweden to Norway. Eventually, we bought our way into the hold of a trawler headed to Iceland. There we found British troops and GIs. From there, we got to New York and to Ellis Island." He turned to stare out at the park. He was a very handsome man, but his features sagged with sadness.

"What an incredible story," I said, genuinely moved. One can hardly imagine what it took to survive St. Petersburg and the onslaught of Barbarossa.

"Yes, it was incredible," he agreed. "It is very painful for me to remember, even more painful to discuss. It was a terrible chapter in human history. But, like so many other immigrants we began again. Nothing like the life we had been accustomed to, but I was able to remedy that with time, hard work, and a great deal of luck.

"But that was so long ago. I prefer to focus on the future---and for me that is my new fascination with your area upstate." Lucius smiled broadly and exclaimed, "What a magnificent place! Totally new to me and absolutely charming. My friend Martha Lee---you know her, surely"---I nodded--- "introduced me to that part of the world and Olana. She suggested I might bring something to the..." He stopped and frowned. " 'Party' isn't quite the right word under the circumstances, is it?"

I grimaced. "No one will ever forget that horrible night at Olana, Lucius. But no one will ever forget the generosity of your gift, either. I think it is marvelous that you want to support Olana. And Martha can be very persuasive. She's a great civic booster."

"Martha! What an intelligent woman! So droll. Coincidentally, when I met her, I was reading an article in the travel section of the *Times* about Olana. I was astounded by the house! A Moorish vision, a fantastic castle that one sees in dreams! Actually, you know, it is not unlike some of our very fanciful 19th century Russian architecture. I look forward to devoting time and resources to such a special house, to sharing my collection of beautiful things."

Paul asked, "Was Sheila part of your collection?"

"I beg your pardon?" Lucius answered sharply.

"We've just seen Dr. Harold Wishman. Sheila had an appointment with him yesterday. He told us you sent Sheila to him. She was planning to get"---Paul searched for the right word---"her bosoms done. Anyone might figure you were taking a pretty personal interest in the woman."

Clearly, Lucius was not pleased.

I said, "Lucius, under the circumstances, you can see why the question had to be asked."

Wrangel's face darkened as he frowned deeply.

"How very unfortunate her death entails such unpleasant intrusions into one's private life. Sheila and I had spent quite a bit of time together in recent weeks arranging for the bequest. We got on famously in what was on my part a strictly avuncular relationship."

"Where did you spend time? At Olana? Here in town?"

"Both here and there. Sheila was a talented, ambitious young woman. Hudson was no longer big enough for her. She desired a larger, more glamorous world. She was like a butterfly emerging from its chrysalis. Yes, I was mildly surprised when she mentioned cosmetic surgery---but heaven knows, many women wish to enhance their appearance. Nor did I find it particularly odd for her to ask my advice on such a thing. Who else could she ask? I suppose Sheila viewed me as a man who is no stranger to personal vanities."

He smiled slightly and put his hand on Paul's shoulder.

"I am flattered, Sheriff, that you imagine a man of my age in a dalliance with someone who could have been my daughter," he laughed brusquely in a mano à mano way, "but please believe me when I tell you her breasts, whatever their size, were of no interest to me personally."

With a glance at me, he continued, "Under the circumstances, I shouldn't be offended by your question. I understand that in a murder investigation, difficult questions have to be asked. Is it appropriate for me to ask what has your investigation yielded thus far?"

Shaking his head, Paul said, "Frankly, not much. The preliminaries are out of the way and all we've got is dead ends. But the investigation is just beginning. I always say, 'It isn't where you start, it's where you finish.'"

Lucius grinned.

"Marvelous expression! And I totally agree. Look at me! And now, alas, my charming guests, I must conclude our visit and return to a very boring array of green visors. Take care, Sheriff," he said, shaking Paul's hand again.

He had apparently sent some sort of signal because the secretary immediately reappeared. Paul headed out through the doors.

"Lindsey," Lucius said, catching my hand, "Huxley tells me you will be joining us for dinner tomorrow. I'll look forward to seeing you then---and to coming to you on the sixth of January, as well. See you upstate."

He kissed my cheek again and I was ushered out.

Beautiful manners. Debonair. Old-world sensibility. I found myself becoming fond of Lucius Wrangel.

Back on the sidewalk I said, "Now what? There's an exhibit I need to see at the Doyle Gallery and I have some follow up to do. What are your plans?"

Paul said, "There has been one development I haven't mentioned to you. We got a call from the Salvation Army in Hudson. They found Sheila's Olana ID tag in the pocket of a pair of jeans somebody turned in. I've got a forensics guy ready to meet me."

"Are you training back?" I asked

"Nah," Paul said. "West Side heliport."

I smiled. "Quite a nice professional courtesy. I don't know the intimate details of your relationship with the current New York City police administration, Paul, but I'd say when you kiss 'em, they stay kissed."

He laughed and said, "See you tomorrow. Try to stay out of trouble."

OFF TO THE DOYLE

Though perhaps not as well known as Sotheby's or Christies, the Doyle Galleries are a superb resource for the decorative arts. Marvelous pieces come to the Doyle throughout the year.

In fact, I first visited the Doyle in the mid-Eighties when they were handling the Count Basie estate. I revered that man! I first danced to his orchestra at a Men's Cotillion and later at a couple of nightclubs when I was in college. So out of sentiment, I went to pay homage, if not to buy. I bought when I began pursuing an interest in certain pieces of estate jewelry and majolica.

Today, there were a couple of Adams style mahogany consoles I needed to examine. They were highly satisfactory and I found other things my clients would appreciate.

What, you ask? To begin with, a set of Dominick & Haff sterling in the Pointed Antique pattern. This was an enormous service for twelve that could take you from morning meals to midnight snacks, through oysters, consommé, two other soups, the fish course, ice cream, fruit, dessert, and demitasse all in one box with everything labeled. There were also some excellent bronzes and several French gilt-metal carriage clocks---I left bids on eight of those. They can be quite scarce sometimes and they look wonderfully dressy in any room.

Many people don't realize that interior designers actually have three jobs. One is to augment taste. The second is to save clients time. Thirdly, is to rent one's expertise; just because something looks real does not mean it is, as they say, The Real McCoy. Lest we taste arbiters become unduly grand, I won't name names but you know who you are, almost every one has some sort of expertise but no one can be an expert on everything. I don't expect my clients to know what I know any more than they expect me to understand securitizing wire transfers or calculating payload for a jumbo jet.

Most interior design assignments don't end with the colors or the proportions of a room, or even the selection of the major pieces of furniture. Increasingly, I find that many clients, especially those who are upgrading lifestyles as well as residences, require all of the accoutrements, the trappings that personalize a house, even though in many cases the act of personalization merely involves the pedestrian act of writing me a check.

Like the portraits of indistinct lineage I mentioned earlier, a new set of china acquired at auction can effortlessly be described as "Grandmother always wanted me to have it." A pair of 19th century bronze figures: "They had been in Uncle Martin's office." The shagreen accessories on the coffee table: "Dad won them in a poker game in Piccadilly during the war." And so on. My old friend Teddy O'Connell once wanted to open an antique store called 'Dead People's Things,' a good name because that's what antiques are---until you buy them.

I was leaving my bids when I heard a voice saying, "It's Fate that has brought us together again!" and turned to find my country neighbor Eleanor Smith standing beside me. I really love Eleanor's taste level and her earthy Texas humor---which only comes out after a glass or two of wine. The stone-cold-sober Eleanor is so proper I fumble for my DAR credentials the minute I see her.

Eleanor uses her maiden name even though she is married to an entrepreneurial charmer named George Donovan. The Donovan-Smiths have been the toast of the valley since about a year ago when they bought a glorious white elephant and have spent a fortune restoring it to its Grand Trianon-like grandeur after the house had endured four decades of savagery at the hands of nuns. Why do so many people leave landmark properties to the Catholic Church? Another important Op-Ed piece waiting to be written.

"I hope you aren't after anything I want," Eleanor said, peering at me over her glasses.

"I hope not, too. What caught your eye, young lady?" I asked after we pecked on cheeks.

"Entirely lighting. We need a chandelier, sconces, even need some plain old table lamps---but come over here and look at these valences." Eleanor hauled me into another room and pointed to four gilded valences, each about four feet long, glorious French rococo. Sublime.

"I can't use 'em but they'd be super in your house," Eleanor chirped.

"Do you think so?" I asked.

"Well, yeah! Hello!? You know they're marvelous!"

"Eleanor," I said, "I'm going to tell you a secret I've never told anyone. Promise me you won't repeat it."

"Go on!" she bleated. "You know I'm trustworthy even when I'm tipsy."

"Window treatments defy me."

It is true. I have never been able to get the hang of draperies. I always let Bennett handle that part of jobs. On the strength of Eleanor's recommendation, I put in a bid on the valences.

"Well, thank heaven our paths are not crossing on the auction floor today. Are you finished here?" I asked. "I had a light lunch but am feeling peckish and could do with some tea or something."

"Excellent idea!" replied Eleanor and we took ourselves off to Gino's.

Gino's is up a block from Bloomingdale's and has the same red and black zebra wall paper that was in El Morocco. The restaurant is one of the few remnants of the old New York when men were men and women ruled from pedestals.

During my first year in New York, I fell in with a group of swells who treated Gino's as their malt shop. Every Friday at one o'clock was a command performance during which Gino himself and his attractive son visited every table and managed the ordering of luncheons as if they were maneuvers in the Normandy invasion. English royalty, movie producers, television and publishing executives, professional athletes, glamorous models, and the ladies who lunch made the scene lively, colorful and amusing. The bar is a tiny affair up front next to the window on Lexington beneath the green striped awning. Eleanor and I sat on stools at the end of the bar and asked for cups of tea. The bartender grimaced as though we had asked for cream of wheat, so we looked at each other, then back at him and ordered white wines.

Leaning close to me, Eleanor whispered, "Huxley tells me you are trying to help figure out who killed that woman at Olana. Is that true?"

I made a mental note to thrash Huxley.

"Not exactly," I hedged. "The sheriff is an old friend I met in New York years ago. He knows I sometimes have good instincts and observe things. There are not very many clues, so we have to lean a lot on motives, psychology. That's where he thinks I could be helpful. For heaven's sake, don't repeat any of this. Huxley shouldn't have said anything in the first place."

Eleanor nibbled a pretzel.

"I didn't really understand the woman. I met her once when she wooed us for the Olana board. I declined. I was appalled ! She wanted to siphon millions of dollars away from worthwhile projects---staving off riverfront developers, for one.

"That idea alone might have been enough of a reason for a serious preservationist to kill her, no kidding."

QUESTIONS AND ANSWERS IN THE VILLAGE

After that one glass of wine, not that you are counting, I dropped Eleanor at Penn Station for her train back to Rhinecliff and continued downtown to my apartment.

My pied à terre in the city is quite a contrast from the house in Hudson. It is the quintessential Village apartment, a modest one-bedroom in a pre-Civil War building.

It also just barely hits 500 square feet if you count the medicine cabinet. I like to say the kitchen was once the glove compartment in a Packard.

The apartment is on the back of the building and is absolutely quiet, a huge plus in New York, but being on the back means it does not enjoy the southern exposure windows of the apartments on the front of the building, and is not flooded with natural light. Were I to sublet it, the headline of the ad would be "No Distracting Glare." Bennett and his grandchildren bounded in one sunny summer day to pick me up for lunch and the boy exclaimed, "Wow! This is like the Bat Cave." Surly little twit.

You may wonder, why am I still here in this small apartment?

I suppose there are several reasons. When I first moved to New York, I indulged my desire to live only in the Village and, as a baby curator, this was what I found and what I could afford. The apartment has a fireplace and is a wonderful winter apartment. It is a block away from three subway lines, it is within walking distance to anything in the Village, Soho or Tribeca, and back then you could hit several of the city's best jazz clubs with a rock. Barney's was four minutes north. Balducci's and the Jefferson Market were down the street. We have no doorman but Horan's, the neighborhood liquor store, receives Fed Ex deliveries, keeps an extra set of keys for unexpected house guests, and pre-ATMs, would deliver a hundred in cash along with the hooch. Many of my neighbors in the early days were born in the neighborhood and told me tales of their youth, the Mom-and-Pop arcades and candy shops, numbers runners and Prohibition high jinks, and I suppose I felt I was making a pilgrimage to the time when the Village was a true Bohemia of eccentric denizens, artists, writers, and bon vivants.

That was not entirely true in the Seventies and even less true now but I will say that the Village still boasts a more colorful and heterogeneous population than the rest of the city.

Nor is the Village as imposing as other neighborhoods. Unlike the canyons of midtown or the opulent facades of grand Upper East Side blocks, the Village has mostly small buildings. This is because the entire area is criss-crossed with underground streams and rivers and does not have the solid bedrock of downtown or uptown to support skyscrapers. Manhattan's rigid street grid of right angles doesn't exist here, either. Like the financial district, the oldest part of town, the Village streets were originally cow paths that meander where they may. At one point down here, 4th Street crosses 12th Street. The small buildings, the narrow winding streets, the simple vernacular architecture are on a more human scale and make the Village, well, a village.

Finally, if you must know, this is a rent-stabilized apartment and after thirty years, the rent has just broken $700. It agrees with my frugal tendencies. Willful waste makes woeful want.

I settled in at my desk and began to make phone calls and send emails.

First, I called Attique. Jim was with a customer but promised to call me back.

Next I sent an email to an old high school chum, Bing Morgan, who does something undoubtedly nefarious down in Langley. As a teenager, Bing was pale, sarcastic, and overweight. He got girls to talk to him by being the class photographer. He and I were on the math team and cemented our friendship in the trenches of trig and calculus. Years after high school, I looked him up in Washington to find he had grown up to be great-looking and handsome in Glen plaid suits. Bing has always been vague about his work in Langley but whatever it is, over the years he has proven to be a superb resource for searching the data bases, government or otherwise, that are continuously being collected about you and me. His immediate email reply said he was calling me and the phone rang.

"Bing! Happy Hollandaise! How's the wife and boy?"

"Happy New Year to you, Lindsey!" After a few moments' pleasantries, he said, "My boy Brian is enrolling in the CIA. That's why I wanted to talk to you."

"Bing, you know a hell of a lot more than I do and I don't even discuss those days."

I could hear him howling. "Not *that* CIA, you paranoid spook!" he laughed. "The Culinary Institute of America. In Hyde Park. He's decided to become a great chef. Since that's just down the road from you, I thought you might know a place he could rent. Might even know somebody with a nice daughter he could meet."

"Ah," I said, "the joke's on me. Have Brian call. I'll give him dinner and put him together with the local realtor---and also check to see if anybody has a spare apartment or barn."

"Great. What do you need to know from Immigration?"

"Name is Lucius Wrangel. Came from Russia via Scandinavia, got to Ellis Island. Probably '42 or '43. I need to know whatever you can find.

Date they arrived, who arrived, ages, whatever. Anything that pops out as newsworthy."

"I'm on it. Ring you back or send by wire. Listen out for Brian's call. Thanks."

I hung up and the phone rang again. It was Paul.

"Hi, my office just got her American Express records. I'm having them forwarded to you now. Let me know what you find. See you tomorrow."

My inbox beeped. I began poring over five years of Sheila's American Express statements.

They showed a lot of Amtrak charges, at least one train each week for most of the year. They also showed that Sheila was a regular customer at some of the better bars and restaurants in town. Maybe she moonlighted for Zagat or reviewed for Gourmet? One of her favorites was the nearby Gotham Bar & Grill, coincidentally one of my preferred haunts. Also the King Cole and the Four Seasons.

This is the kind of field work I was born to do.

I hustled over to Gotham in advance of the cocktail hour, easily claimed a stool at the bar and began chatting with Fritz, my favorite bartender, who makes one of the best Manhattans in Manhattan. Fritz marinates his cherries in Grand Marnier, too divine. Fritz is also revolted by flavored vodkas; he says the category may be going through the roof but for us purists, it's another sign of the end of civilization as we know it. He and his family have a cottage in the Catskills so we also have the country in common.

"Greetings, noble sire," I hailed Fritz, elegant in his silk patterned vest. "I come in search of a mystery woman."

"You just missed her. She asked if I knew any nice girls and I thought of you."

"Naughty Fritz!" I laughed. "You know my heart belongs to Mayor Bloomberg, if only he'd call me."

Fritz placed my delicious cocktail in front of me and brought over a bowl of nuts. I selected a filbert, held it up and asked, "What has a brain this size and chairs the House?"

Fritz smiled ruefully. "Cheers. To your health and the health of the Republic."

"Ever see this woman?" I asked, handing him a picture of Sheila.

"Yeah, she's a customer. Comes in a few times a month. Has a drink, then meets someone for dinner."

"Anybody in particular?"

"Different guys. Usually an older fellow. Beard. Nice looking. Sharp dresser. "

"Is this the fellow?"

He took the picture of Wrangel. "Yep, I've seen him."

We returned to conversation on politics, his children's little league, last summer's millipede invasions, and the Yankees' pitching rotation. I said I'd see him soon and left to get a cab uptown.

The King Cole Bar at the St. Regis is dominated by Maxfield Parrish's ribald mural of the monarch, bemused on his throne, flanked by his jesters. In the seventies---when midtown was my stomping ground---I was a regular. Back then though, the bar was in an adjacent area of the hotel and was a vast room with thirty foot ceilings. It had a mezzanine for drinks looking down on a dining room filled with big, circular, brown leather banquettes and facing chairs. In the center of each banquette, a six foot dried or fresh floral arrangement changed according to the seasons. The waiters were dressed in costumes of King Cole's era, brown tights and deep green doublets. Sort of Robin Hood's merry men with cocktail shakers. The mural reposed above the bar which stretched the length of the wall opposite the mezzanine. Why that room vanished, none of us will ever understand. It was replaced by a plush, dark, run-of-the-midtown rectangle crowded with people talking too loudly, and, I understand, prostitutes on weekday nights for the out-of-towners. I suppose they relocated while the Oak Bar was closed. Plus ça change, plus ça mort d'esprit.

I hit the drinks hour squarely. Financial types were already three deep at the bar, talking too loudly.

I stood around for a few minutes, knowing that a still attractive woman in the shank of youth was not going to be offered a seat when, to my astonishment, a man turned and said, "Why don't you sit here, miss? My friends may not have any manners, but I do."

Thanking him, I sprang onto the stool and watched for the barkeep. When he arrived I said, "I'll have a Perrier and I need to ask you a question." Looking at the picture, he said Sheila came in regularly, met a guy and left.

James at the Four Seasons gave me pretty much the same story. Came in, had a drink or two. Met a guy for dinner. Identified the photograph. James then told me I was a lousy customer, never came in any more. With a pledge to rectify that oversight, I left, suddenly inspired by an idea.

I took a cab to Lucius Wrangel's apartment building on Fifth in the eighties. It is said in New York that there really are only two kinds of apartment buildings; those with Puerto Rican doormen and those with Irish doormen. This one was Irish.

"Good evening, young man," I said with a smile. "I wonder if you could help me. I'm a private investigator trying to find a missing person. A young lady. She disappeared from her grandmother's co-op in this area. Do you recognize her?" I showed the picture of Sheila.

"Oh, sure. That's Mr. Wrangel's secretary. She comes by every week or so. She's missing?" he asked, alarmed.

"What?!" I said, taking back the picture. "Oh, silly me. That's not the picture. That's Mr. Wrangel's secretary. *This* is the missing girl," and showed him a picture of myself taken in Huxley's back yard last summer.

"Nah. Never seen her. Sorry."

By the time I got home, I was starving and the message light on phone was flashing.

Bennett had called to say the clivia was budding and that he was out for the evening, dining in Red Hook, but would ring back later.

Jim from Attique had called and left his home number for me to call back.

When he answered I said, "I'm investigating price-fixing in the used bathtub market."

He replied, "Hello, Lindsey."

"I truly am doing research on one of your customers. Do you recall a Lucius Wrangel?"

"Yep." Nothing if not laconic.

"He told me he purchased a Mexican painting from you that had a Frederic Church behind it."

"The new Church portrait that's getting all the press? Why would I sell that for $250?"

"Petit mal? Pre-Christmas clearance? You tell me."

"Well, I do remember him and I do remember the painting he bought. Guadalajara primitive. I guarantee there was no Church behind it."

"How can you be so sure?"

"Because things shifted around in that container on the way up here and there was some damage. The frame splintered on one corner. I had to replace it, did it myself. I also had to stretch the canvas again, so I can guarantee there was just the one picture. Sounds like you got the runaround, dear. However, we have a nice shipment coming in from Egypt next week with very tasty Tutankhamen temperas behind Farouk campaign posters. I'll save one for you. "

"Thank you, James. I'll take two."

CVS and Bank Records

Before heading back upstate the next morning, I spent a few more hours in town scouting around for Canton.

A new client has bought a delightful colonial Dutch cottage in the village of Livingston. The dining room has the characteristic built-in corner cupboards and, since she already has the beginnings of a collection of blue and white, we decided acquiring a few more pieces would be a pretty solution. The porcelain would display beautifully in that room---and would also be an excellent investment.

I first became acquainted with Canton, Chinese export ware, when I was in college. My art history advisor and her husband had a marvelous collection. 'Canton' refers to the city of origin, now Guangzhou. Chinese porcelain began to be exported to America in the 17th century and the trade became truly brisk in the 18th and 19th centuries, peaking about 1860. The blue and white porcelain, also known as 'ballast ware' because it came to America in the holds of the sailing ships, was a great favorite with colonial society---Washington, Jefferson, and Hamilton all had tea and dinner services---and is highly collectible today. Every piece of Canton is unique, not only because each was hand-painted but because there is such a range of colorations. Depending upon the amount of pigment and the firing heat, the colors can range from soft bluish gray to cobalt.

Canton is painted exclusively with rural scenes, usually willow trees surrounding a tea house and perhaps an arched bridge over a quiet stream. There may be mountains in the distance. People are never present, only nature. The porcelain is quite simple and rustic. Rims may not be quite symmetrical and the surfaces not entirely smooth. Blue and white is altogether charming because each plate, bowl, or platter is a little piece of history.

If you decide to shop for ballast ware, be aware that in 1890 the U.S. Government trade office insisted 'China' or 'Made in China' be painted on the underside, so the older pieces of Canton are unmarked as they arrived with paper labels.

Among Canton collectors, a tureen is the Holy Grail. If you run across one, please call me immediately.

Today, I found a few pieces at the antiques building in Chelsea and a couple of others at a tiny little hole in the wall shop behind a tailor in the Korean district. That done, I headed home.

I just made the 11:30 Adirondack, arrived in Hudson two hours later, picked up my car at the station and drove directly to the drug store for scrips and sundries.

For my entire adult life I have bought cosmetics only at Saks Fifth Avenue---and fragrance only in Europe. Did you realize French perfumes sold here have different formulations?

Caveat emptor, honey.

But, as the flesh begins to fall away from the bone, I find myself taking any opportunity to shore up the old epidermis and that includes looking for miracle face creams on drug store shelves. I don't do it when I am with other people and I certainly wouldn't do it if I saw you there.

When I am in CVS or Duane Reade, I scrutinize the L'Oreal, Roc, and Olay ingredients and their claims that I will look myself at twenty-five after a fortnight's use. I once tried La Mer but therein, I fear, lies the road to ruin. There is precious little point in a single woman being beautiful if she is penniless. Most days I frugally opt for the four dollar generic vitamin E cream.

Today, however, I decided to spend $21.99 for something that not only said it would visibly reduce wrinkles in fifteen minutes but had excellent copy promising *lift*. That is what most women are living for now---*lift*. I have almost delayed too long in making my London debut but now that I have this cream, and will shortly have lift, perhaps I should go forward with my plans.

Clutching my emollient, I rounded the corner toward the pharmacist and ran into an acquaintance lurking in the pedal abrasion section.

"What have we here!" I crowed. "Stefan Sheridan, the famous interior designer!"

Stefan is in *Architectural Digest* every other issue, having done some star's digs in the Hollywood Hills, or a film tycoon's manse in Bel Air, to say nothing of numerous Park Avenue penthouses and several restorations up here.

Stefan's origins are humble---born in Ohio to a family that managed self-storage facilities and laundromats. To pay his way through college, he and three friends painted pirate murals for a motel chain's bars, drawing straws each morning to decide who would paint foreground, background, or faces. He got his big designing break when he came to New York and was hired by Radio City to work on sets for the pageants. Stefan calls that phase of his career Holiday on Wood. I loved his neon crèche. His papier mâche Red Sea parting and the Rockettes' flight from Egypt were triumphs.

Stefan evidently owns an entire armoire of black turtlenecks since that's all he wears, paired with black jeans or safari shorts and that gorgeous blond hair. He's bicoastal, has a great eye, and everyone who knows him loves him. Let's face it---lots of decorators are snooty but Stefan's ability to work and play well with others gets him lots of repeat business and, as I said, copious spreads in coffee table books.

After our three cheek kisses, I said, "I saw the piece on that big shot's place you did in Palm Springs. Great infinity pool."

Stefan waved one hand in the air, placed the other on his hip and said, "Infinity itself will have to pass before I ever work with that man again." He then volunteered, "You are probably wondering what the Olana murder means to me."

"This very morning I asked myself that question," I replied. "And the answer is…?"

"One commission down el draino. Sheila planned to redo her lodgings and had hired me to supply the appropriate taste level."

"You mean her place in Kinderhook?" I asked.

"No, no, nooooo! The swell little spot she had just bought on 67th off Madison."

My jaw dropped. "Using what for money?"

"Ah!" he said. "That was what I wondered." After leaving me with that little tidbit, Stefan departed with two boxes of Clairol Tawny Gold and a box of Russell Stover turtles he said were for his housekeeper.

I was headed for the car when my phone rang. Paul announced Sheila's financial records had arrived and instructed me to appear in his office *tout suite* to review them.

Based on Stefan's news bulletin, I said, "I just got some incredible news! Sheila had a new address!"

"Honey," he said, "you have no idea."

Paul and I spent an hour hunkered down at his desk looking at sheaves of statements from half a dozen checking, money market, and brokerage accounts. Neither of us was prepared for what we found. Paul called Ted Marks.

"Ted, Paul Whitbeck. Lindsey and I need to drop by for a quick visit. See you in five."

We walked through the front door of the law offices of Curry, Curry, Marks and Quinn. Ted Marks appeared in a dark gray flannel suit, looking much better than he had during his initial interview.

We went into his office and sat around a small conference table since his desk was covered with books and files. Paul got out his glasses and perched them on his nose. Placing several fat manila folders on the table, he said, "What we have here are Sheila's bank records we subpoenaed.

Before we get into them, let me ask you a couple of questions. Did Sheila have a will?"

Ted shook his head.

"None that I am aware of. Neither of us does…. did. But that's not unusual. Most people our age don't plan to die any time soon and haven't gotten around to a will."

Paul nodded. "Just wanted to be clear on that. According to the laws of New York State, if a wife dies without a will the husband inherits, have I got that right?" Paul asked.

Ted Marks spoke sharply, "Yes, you've got that right. But why is that of any consequence? There's the house, which we owned together. We've got joint checking and savings accounts. No big surprises there. Sheila was well paid but neither her salary nor mine is, or was, anything like big money. For God's sake, Paul, get to the point. What do you want? I have other things on my mind." Ted pushed his chair away from the table.

"In a hurry, are you, Ted Marks?" Paul asked, leaning forward. He switched to a gentler, more solicitous tone. "Maybe you need to take a little vacation. After all, you've had a big shock."

"As a matter of fact, I am planning to go away for a few days."

"Any place special?"

"New Hampshire. Do a little skiing. Just get out of town for a bit. I've been on the wagon for a few days now and I like it. I feel like a new man. Or a new widower."

Paul slowly stood and began deliberately pacing back and forth across the office, continuing to ask questions. "Have you thought about taking a nice cruise? Get a boat, take it around the Caribbean? Maybe look at some real estate, find a nice place for your retirement. No since waiting 'til the last minute."

Paul's sarcasm was not lost me and certainly not on Ted Marks.

"What are you getting at?" he asked, his voice rising.

Paul turned and leaned across the desk close to Ted's face.

"What I'm getting at, Mr. Marks, is even though, as you say, your joint accounts are nothing to brag about, your wife had other accounts. One account has slightly over two million dollars. You are her inheritor. Are you honestly going to tell me you knew nothing about that?"

Ted Marks jaw dropped in what appeared to be genuine surprise.

"Two million dollars?"

"Yep. And you may own the house in Kinderhook jointly, but last month Sheila closed on an apartment in New York. Any idea what that address might be?" Paul cocked his head waiting for an answer.

Marks looked first at me, then at Paul. He seemed bewildered.

"I don't know anything about any apartment," he said, loosening his tie. "Where'd you get the idea she owned an apartment?"

"Your accounts up here were pin money!" Paul snapped. "Sheila kept her serious finances *and* a safe deposit box in the city."

He began pulling documents from the files and slamming them on the table.

"Here's the apartment deed. Here's the brokerage statement. Two checking accounts." He passed them across the desk to Ted, then leaned back in his chair watching closely as Ted looked at the documents.

The sheriff said, "You look like a man who's maybe going to need a lawyer, counselor."

ON TO TROY

After we left Ted and were walking back to Paul's office, I asked Paul what he planned to do with the bombshell on Sheila's finances.

"The first thing is to talk to the accounting firm who does Olana's books. Don't forget---she had access to all the funds."

"Are you saying it was embezzlement? That's too much money to get away with."

"She has two million in the bank. It had to come from somewhere and there's a safe around the corner from her office. That has to be the first place to look. Sugar daddies, money laundering, and drugs will have to wait until tomorrow."

We called Olana's accounting firm in Troy to say we were on our way. As we drove up I-87 at a hundred miles an hour, not in his Jeep but in a police sedan with lights flashing, Paul gave me a run-down on what was wrong with local, state, and national government, and a colorful earful on Brian Cashman's sins. In short order we were moving into the heart of downtown Troy.

In the late 19th century, thanks to detachable shirt collar, cuff, and bosom makers, as well as iron works, Troy was one of the richest cities in America, overshadowing Albany, the state capital across the river. Its Victorian charm is terribly down at heel now but some enterprising soul is going to make an absolute killing in real estate there because, like Hudson, Troy has a wealth of architectural heritage. Downtown has block after block of handsome stores, shops, brownstones and apartment buildings, all preserved because no one in the 20th century had the money to tear them down and rebuild. Acres of brick warehouses and factories, many along the banks of the river, stand empty, ready to be converted to lofts. There are exceptionally fine residential areas from the 19th century, ornate town houses and maisonettes in various stages of dilapidation and disrepair, many built around private squares and gardens like Gramercy Park, and more Tiffany windows per square mile than anywhere else in the world.

I could tell when we walked into the accounting firm's offices this was not going to be a typical Big Eight afternoon. The reception area was furnished with early American reproductions from High Point circa 1995. Add to that miles of plastic moldings and circular ceiling motifs from which hung Home Depot chandeliers. Several paintings by that Kinkeade fellow hung on the walls, illuminated by pin lights. I felt abysmal but Paul bristled with the confidence that he was about to nail an embezzler.

Two partners, a man and a woman, emerged to greet us effusively and escort us into a conference room. The woman was wearing an aggressive blue dress which screamed half sizes and the man was wearing a suit I could have sworn came from Robert Hall. He had a diamond ring on one hand, a huge class ring on the other, and a Rolex as big as a hubcap. She wore an ankle bracelet.

Both were affable until Paul explained that we were going to need to examine all their files on Olana because we suspected a substantial sum might have wandered off.

This produced a great deal of sputtering that included, "Absolutely impossible! Scrupulous record keeping! Audit them every year! Highly professional! Constantly upgrading systems and oversight!"

"How difficult would it be for someone to embezzle money?" I asked.

They spoke as one. "Virtually impossible."

Paul handed them his card and said, "Have everything to my office by tomorrow morning or I'll have you in court tomorrow afternoon."

◆◆◆◆◆

The sun was gone when we finally got to Olana.

When we suddenly appeared at the door of Eve Healy's office, she was startled.

"Is something wrong? I'm surprised to see you."

Paul said, "We need to tie up some loose ends. Take us through your banking procedures again, would you? Especially the part about who makes the deposits."

"I make all the deposits."

"And you disburse funds," I said. "How many signatures are required on a check?"

Eve's face reddened. "Are you accusing me of stealing?"

"No, but we do have reason to think there may be some money missing," Paul said.

"But these questions! You think someone was embezzling! You think it was me!" She put her head down on her desk and began to cry. After a few moments of listening to her sob, I pressed my handkerchief into one of her hands, walked behind her, and put my hands gently on her shoulders.

"Eve," Paul said. "Just talk to us."

I brought her a glass of cold water.

Gradually she stopped crying. Lifting her head, Eve said bitterly, "You cannot imagine how glad I am she's dead. I had just come to work here. I wasn't paid very much. My daughter had an accident and needed surgery. My health insurance wasn't in effect yet and I didn't have the money. Sheila was so sympathetic. She said Olana would make me a loan from funds, told me to withdraw whatever I needed and pay it back over time. It never occurred to me there was anything odd about it. I thought she could do whatever she wanted."

"There was nothing in writing about a loan?" Paul asked.

"No. I withdrew the five thousand I needed and used it to pay for the hospital. Later, she came to me and said that it would appear that I had stolen the money."

"Didn't it occur to you to simply tell someone about this?" I suggested.

"It would have been my word against hers. I thought I had done something illegal. In retrospect, I realize that was asinine, but at the time I was pretty green. And the withdrawal would still have been on the books, even though...even though..." She began to sob again. "Even though I repaid it."

♦ ♦ ♦ ♦ ♦

Paul and I reviewed the day over a glass of wine at the Red Dot, the saloon on Warren Street where the dregs and the dukes of Hudson meet. A few doors down from the Opera House, the Red Dot is painted taupe with dark red shutters. The blinds on the windows are permanently at half mast. The Dot began as a long dark room with a bar against one wall and tables too close for comfort. At some point it expanded into an L-shaped space to accommodate more dining but the cocktail hour is the Dot's raison d'etre.

If you are interested in who's buying, selling, or remodeling, or need to find a mason, a plumber, or an electrician, the Red Dot bar is the right place from five o'clock onward. At drinks, truckers stand along side antique dealers, realtors next to welfare cases, gallery owners next to mafiosos from across the river. It's a potpourri but it's a snapshot of our little burg.

Paul and I sat at one end of the bar avoiding others' overtures for conversation and reflecting. Sipping a pinot noir he said, "Looks like another dead end. But, even after that sob story, should we believe that Eve wasn't in on the embezzlement with Sheila? Or that she didn't kill her? That woman is over six feet tall, big enough to go bear hunting with a switch. She could have wrung Sheila's little blonde neck in no time. I'm surprised she hadn't done it years ago. What a mean thing to do! Lady needs an operation for her little girl and winds up getting blackmailed. I don't know about you, but I'm not missing Sheila."

I stared into my wine. "The accounting records will tell the tale, but I honestly cannot see how anyone could have embezzled a few million dollars. Even if Sheila and Eve were working together. Even if the accountants look like dunderheads. It's too much money to get away with. There has to be another angle."

I drove home and arrived to find Bennett sitting in my living room reading. As I walked in, he stood and looked pointedly at his watch.

"I have drawn a bath for you. Some time ago it had bubbles. I suspect they are now flat. You have about eight minutes to enjoy what was to be a leisurely soak before we drive down to Huxley. You look tired. Still a lovely creature," he took my coat, "but a bit tired, Madame.

"Have we had luck in the murder department? Do we wish a dressing drink?"

I sank into a chair and kicked off my shoes. "Yes, I suppose I could have a small glass of wine. Huxley won't be delirious if we're a minute late.

"As for the murder department? The autopsy featured a doctor who's James Mason one minute and Casanova the next. Sheila's assistant is panting for the widower Marks whose alibi is holding firm. Today I learned Sheila just bought an apartment in the city and has two million dollars in the bank."

Bennett mused aloud, "Dear me! Whence her source of coins, one wonders?"

"Exactly. I can't fathom how she could siphon that amount of money out of Olana undetected. Then we have all those trips into the city. She must have been wooing more than donors for her building project. There must be a man in the picture."

Bennett nodded. "Indubitably, Madame. I'd go with the Sugar Daddy theory."

Huxley's Dinner Party

As Bennett drove us down to Huxley's, I pondered.

Van der Wyck's professional jealousy. Eve's hungering for advancement, loving Ted, *and* feeling she could be black-mailed. Martha's vindictiveness. The spurned husband. All time-honored, so to speak, reasons for murder. Baroness James's Dalgliesh once observed only the four L's are motives for murder: Love. Lust. Lucre. Loathing. Sheila's marriage was loveless. Ted inherited a small fortune. Lust lurked. As for loathing, she was abundantly, actively disliked. Perhaps, like Caesar, Sheila was killed by committee?

The 'how' problem also remained. How was a woman strangled in a house teeming with people preparing for a party? Sheila had been conspicuously present shortly before guests began arriving. Caterers and wait staff were all over the house. A docent meeting was held at the last minute with women in every room upstairs. Men were hauling in the painting and setting it up. However the murder happened, it must have been fast work. Had someone hired a professional, I wondered?

These thoughts flew around in my head like bats as we turned into Huxley's drive.

Slipping into the house through the side porch, Bennett and I came through the laundry room and kitchen to find everyone at the bar where

Huxley's attorney, Jerome Morgenthau, was holding forth on the proper way to make a Negroni. Wines were being poured and introductions made in an extremely jovial atmosphere. When we had secured our potions of choice, we paraded off en masse to the living room babbling and laughing, Achilles preceding us at a brisk pace.

The living room is just as it was thirty years ago when Huxley's decorator, who also worked for the Duchess of Windsor and Bobby Short, just to give you a rough idea of tone, had created an essentially chartreuse parlor to compliment Huxley's late wife Helène's red hair. The room is highly ornamental, accented with majolica, oriental vases, and one extremely dead corn plant which Bennett deftly stashed behind a Chinese screen before anyone spotted it.

The windows on the wall facing the river are framed by exquisite striped silk draperies in citrus shades---their treble swags and tiebacks are worthy of an opera. Six enormous botanical prints of fritillaria, framed in citrine faux bamboo, hang on one wall opposite a wonderful stained wood and painted parchment cabinet inlaid with hammered copper and pewter by that most effete, extraordinary and under-appreciated turn-of-the-century Italian designer, Carlo Bugatti. A marble bust of Robert Fulton peered down from high in one corner of the room and Pascal peered from another.

The room has several conversation groupings. This evening Huxley had situated us across the southern half of the room in an arrangement of soft chintz sofas and chairs with hors d'oeuvres trays placed on the coffee table and occasional tables.

As usual, Huxley had assembled an interesting group for dinner. Most evening entertaining in the country involves dinner parties in people's houses. Hardly anyone goes out to dinner because there are not that many decent places, not counting Gigi's, the local version of the Stork Club.

We were a party of ten.

Eleanor Smith, whom you've met, and her husband, George Donovan.

Lucius was chatting with Bennett and two playwrights in an animated way, leaning forward with elbows on his knees. He looked sharp in a dark blazer with a pocket crest and a harlequin silk square, a white shirt open at the neck, charcoal trousers, and gleaming loafers.

Huxley had invited another Russian émigré friend, Katerina Schaefer, to meet Lucius and she sat to his left, bundled in a Fair Isle sweater topped somewhat incongruously with a purple Fortuny scarf.

Huxley's agent, Jerome Morgenthau, who is always mentioned in the press when one Hollywood studio buys another, wore a red v-neck and gray flannel trousers and sat between Katerina and Huxley's neighbor, Margaret Windly, she of the poultry Windlys, who as far as I can tell spends her days solely occupied with raising prize chickens.

The two upholstered club chairs flanking our host held the playwrights, two men who are adapting 'Mommie Dearest' as a musical.

Aside from Margaret, who had brought Huxley a lovely Shaker basket of green and blue eggs from her highly-pedigreed hens---"I'm not giving you that basket, Hux, just the eggs"-- all the women were wearing dark slacks and bright sweaters or sport coats with dressy scarves, except for Eleanor Smith, who always wears black.

Margaret, now seventy-ish I suppose, still a very svelte and handsome woman who must have been a stunner in her earlier days, was certainly the most well-turned out in a long camel cashmere skirt and matching cowl neck sweater belted in alligator. Her still vaguely blonde curly hair flounced attractively and she had taken more than usual care with her makeup. Could she be setting her cap for Huxley, I wondered?

Huxley sported his favorite sweater, a jewel-tone cardigan a neighbor, Francesca Orloff, had knitted for him and dark green cords with a jade green silk shirt. As usual, he wore no shoes but shuffled around in a pair of red socks.

The theatrical pair in the club chairs were bonding merrily with Lucius. The pug cavorted happily, eagerly suggesting his interest in a cracker or smoked oyster. James Abbott, the writer, wore a navy suit and a white t-shirt with black sneakers. His partner, Philip Brashear, sported an Indian tunic and---well, I can only say harem pants.

I sat down on the couch at the end of the room between George and Eleanor. The Donovan-Smiths are about my age and must be rich as Croesus, though no one has figured out quite how, and are what I would describe as a happily married team. Both are southerners, a plus in my opinion, and are endlessly charming.

Naturally everyone was eager to hear about the authors' progress in setting Joan Crawford to music.

"We see her story as the age-old struggle for female primacy in a man's world," asserted James Abbott, the librettist and writer of the book. "This is leavened by the eats-her-young intrigue."

"Whom do you see in the lead?" asked agent Morgenthau, who represents a lot of actors.

Huxley offered, "I just can't see Julia as Joan, can you?"

"What about Gwyneth?" someone suggested.

"Oh, God, no!" Huxley moaned. "She's like one of those Kabuki dolls. Only has that one expression---frozen concern. I'd sooner see Queen Latifah."

George Donovan leaned forward and called out to Abbott, "Whoever you cast, I'm here to tell you to save us all seats on opening night. I'm going to write down my name and give it to you because when the curtain goes up, I want to be there!" and as an aside to me, "along with every fag on five continents."

"What about Jackie?" I said, to a resounding chorus of 'Jackie who?'

"Bisset, of course," I replied. "One of the great talents of our generation."

Everyone smiled. I am constantly proposing Jackie Bisset for one role or another. She is so brilliant and yet so under appreciated.

Abbott continued, "We haven't decided how to handle the aging process."

"Who the hell has?" everyone shouted.

"It will be difficult to find one actress who can take Crawford from her teens through the Pepsi Cola era. And, in fact, it might be better for box office if we had a different lead in each of the three acts. What would you think about that?"

"Cate Blanchett?"

"No, I've been leery of her ever since 'Hedda Gabler'. The best thing that could be said about *that* performance was thank heaven she had a second pistol."

Gesturing to me to refill wine glasses, Huxley said, "Children, please! Obviously it should be Lindsay Lohan in Act I, Patty Lupone in Act II, and Brad Pitt in Act III. He hasn't done any cross-dressing yet. It's breakthrough."

"If you can get the wigs right, the rest of it will take care of itself," said Eleanor. "Is Sidney Guilaroff still with us?"

"Unfortunately not. He first did Joan Crawford's hairstyles in 'The Ice Follies of 1939.' That man did everybody."

"Just like you," Abbott muttered to his partner.

Lucius remarked, "How refreshing to look forward to a totally new production. Broadway seems to exist only on revivals these days."

Huxley wailed, "How true! In fact, we're having revivals of revivals. Any moment now someone will combine *Gypsy* and *Oklahoma* and restage it as *Ethel Get Your Gun.*"

He stood and began walking toward the kitchen. "Never fear. I am going to feed you. I'll be back."

There ensued debate and discussion on the fate of satire, real estate, the cost of hotels in European capitals, and the New York Yankees' prospects for the spring. George moved to sit next to Margaret and flirted shamelessly. Eleanor joined the playwrights to find out who was producing their new work and ask about sitting in on rehearsals. Bennett and Morgenthau were lamenting the electrical systems in their old Jaguars. I heard snatches of several conversations, someone's life being described as 'so dull he's living for his spam' and 'she's had them done twice already but the third time's the charm' and 'you cannot believe the asking price and they aren't even allowed to paint the shutters.'

"Lindsey," Katerina came over and sat beside me. "Your friend Lucius---is that his name?---seems to have a curious idea of fashion. Who would wear a Romanov crest?" I suddenly realized Katerina had had perhaps one more glass of wine than was absolutely necessary.

"Well," I pointed out, "he is from Russia."

"Frigging czarist," she muttered.

Huxley reappeared and beckoned us to dinner.

We were arrayed around Huxley's splendid round walnut table. The dining room was lit entirely by candles in the chandelier and sconces on both sideboards and the mantle. I don't need to tell you how flattering that lighting is. George took the brass blowpoke, rearranged the fire slightly, and threw on another log while Huxley busied himself seating us, boy-girl, boy-girl.

The table was set with chargers and colorful over-wide ceramic bowls. Dinner was to be a simple affair. Huxley and his crock pot are culinary wonders. He has single-handedly revived national interest in short ribs of beef, presented tonight in a succulent, rich sauce with just a touch of tamari and accompanied by freshly baked biscuits and an avalanche of arugula.

Katerina at her pompous if slightly slurred best began early to establish her Russian bona fides.

"Lucius!" she snapped. "What was your last name again?"

"Wrangel, Madame," he answered and inclined his head toward her in a courtly way.

"Are you related to *the* Baron Wrangel?" she inquired.

"We are---or were," Lucius replied. "He died some years before I was born. He was my father's first cousin."

"He was a White Russian." Katerina observed. "Are your people White Russians?" Just a hint of a hiccup there.

"Indeed, Madame."

"So you come from a family of Czarists!" she cried. "Fans of dear Nicholas' crowned, empty head. I suppose you dismiss the revolution?"

"Would that one could dismiss it," replied Lucius gravely.

"You would have clung to the czar?" she asked, in mock astonishment. "The czar and his nobles ruling a nation of superstitious serfs?

Lenin and Stalin gave the peasants schools! Created a literate generation! The czar wanted the people to remain slaves!"

"And Lenin and Stalin did not?" Lucius asked patiently.

"The czar censored the press."

"And Lenin and Stalin did not?" Lucius asked again.

Katerina persisted in being provocative. "People who were not Russian Orthodox---we Jews, of course---suffered in the czar's pogroms."

Lucius paused for several uncomfortable moments. Eventually he answered in measured tones.

"May I ask, dear Kharechka,"---I thought his addressing her in the familiar was a good sign given her belligerence---"where is your family from?"

"We lived in Moscow. But our family home, our roots, were in Odessa."

"Ah yes, Odessa. A city more European than Russian. The pearl of the Black Sea.

"I described my parents as White Russians to differentiate them from the Romanovs' assassins. My parents were not interested in any ideology. Not that of the royalists, certainly not the mob rule of the Bolsheviks. My father was an architect and engineer. My mother managed our estates. Their closest friends were artists in the early movement, *Mir Iskusstva* ---the World of Art group."

"Yes," said Katerina. "The Russian art nouveau."

"Exactly. Early abstract art that led to Constructivism, Supremativism, early Cubism. My parents' friends included Malevich, Soutine, Pevsner, and later Kandinsky, Chagall, and Archipenko. Yes, they all argued constantly about ideologies---but only philosophies of art. When Lenin became premier, the radical energy of the avant-garde was replaced by the solemn grandeur of Soviet realism. As the climate became perilous, the artists fled to Europe and America. My father always said he should have gone then, too. But love of country is strong."

What had begun as typical dinner party intellectual tit for tat seemed to be escalating. Katerina's anger was building.

"That is the symbol of the czar!" she exclaimed, pointing at the gold embroidered standard on Lucius' blazer. "A symbol of nobility! Not the hammer and sickle of the peasants!"

Several of us exchanged looks that said, Would somebody please change the subject!

"Katerina," Lucius said, with a friendly pat on her outstretched arm, "you surprise me with your paean to the hammer and sickle."

She persisted. "That crest gave the people nothing. Stalin gave them a constitution and the right to vote." She tossed down her remaining wine.

"Katerina. My dear ingénue. Stalin's constitution, proclaimed 'the most democratic in the world,' was a sham. He enforced dictatorship with secret police and state terror."

Katerina said, "He collectivized the farms, taking land from the nobility to feed the people."

Bennett spoke up. "The collectives were a colossal failure. Two million died of starvation in the Ukraine alone. In Odessa, Katerina. You must have heard this from your own family."

Bravely trying to distract Katerina, George Donovan asked loudly, "Has anybody been to the Russian night clubs in Coney Island?"

Katerina reached for the wine bottle. "The women loved him! He gave them jobs equal to their husbands! He gave them hospitals to have their babies!"

Morgenthau interjected, "Stalin even gave the women medals for motherhood."

She countered, "We needed children to replace dead soldiers!"

"And to replace those eliminated in his purges," Lucius answered. "Ten million people were eradicated by Stalin, the little cobbler's son."

I said, "Lucius, tell us when you escaped."

"By 1940, when Trotsky was assassinated with a Mexican ice pick, my parents knew they had to get out and made plans to emigrate to America. Stalin was unprepared for Hitler's invasion, even though U.S. spies had warned him, as had Churchill. In retrospect, I'm sure he felt he'd been overzealous in purging 40,000 officers. Then the siege began. For two years we were trapped in St. Petersburg ."

Katerina insisted on having the last word. "Stalin's industrialization saved Britain and the U.S. Without Stalin, the Nazi war machine would have won. Is that sufficient justification for you?"

I couldn't believe Lucius held his temper in the face of her idiotic barrage. Like the rest of us, I was relieved when Huxley burst in, "Katerina! For God's sake! You are no longer being an agent provocateur! You're being ridiculous! I'm sending you—no, I'm *taking* you to the gulag!"

The table erupted in nervous laughter.

"Come Comrade Katerina! Help me with dessert. "

Katerina looked addled and embarrassed.

She said, "Yes, Huxley. I have gotten carried away."

Lucius graciously said, "Katerina is right, of course. We must always welcome change. At dessert we will discuss the *American* revolution---the next one!" Everyone applauded, much relieved that Katerina's tirade had ended without scimitars being drawn.

Lucius walked to Katerina and held her chair as she stood to follow Huxley. "Come, my dear," he said. "I will escort you."

We all exhaled.

"Jesu!" exclaimed Margaret Windly. "I didn't realize that was a Russian crest he was wearing. What an explosion!"

"Katerina enjoys sounding off," Morgenthau allowed. "You should have seen her in her youth. When she first came to New York, she couldn't decide whether to be a Bolshevik or a Beatnik. She got a job with Condé Nast that sorted out her priorities. You can't be a communist if you work for Vogue."

Lucius and Katerina reappeared bearing dessert plates which they put on the sideboard. Huxley followed them bearing a chocolate torte and a bowl of crème fraiche.

Huxley said, "I've put coffee on. Why don't we go outside for an intermezzo?" The pug who had been lying by the fire ran barking to the French doors.

We all trooped out to the back porch for a breath of air and to admire the mountains and the star-filled night sky.

We watched a barge moving slowly past on the river far below Huxley's lawn and I remarked, "I hear in the spring the Hudson Dayliners are coming back."

These were the enormously popular sightseeing boats that ran between Hudson and New York in the early years of the 20th century. Great wooden steamships with names like *Cornelius, Liberty,* and *Hendrick Hudson* carried courting couples, picnicking families, city people hungry for a breath of fresh air, and tourists in scenic journeys that took an entire day---or sometimes two---to towns along the Hudson and back to New York.

"The Dayliners! I remember them so vividly as a child," Lucius exclaimed.

"Shortly after we arrived and had gotten established, my father booked passage for us as a special treat. What wonderful trips! Great ships still at Hudson's docks. So many small stations along the way---Greendale, Barrytown, Rokeby. The grand sweep of the Highlands. West Point, where they told us the story of Washington's troops putting a chain across the Hudson to stop the British. Cruising past the Palisades and Spuyten Duyvil. The canyons of New York.

"As a little boy, I raced around on deck catching the spray of the waves while my father sat in his jacket and straw boater and my mother in a long frock. We were so happy to have made a new beginning. Those were heady trips for a young immigrant. The scenery! Sailboats drawing past us! The great Hudson River and its Valley! I have never forgotten those rides."

Shortly, after our host and companions had retreated to the warmth of Huxley's dining room fireplace and Lucius and I were alone, I asked, "Why are you being coy about the painting?"

" 'Coy?' What an odd word, my dear."

"By 'coy,' I mean Church's portrait of the young woman did not come from Attique, as you very well know."

Lucius laughed and put his arm around my shoulder, giving me a hug. "Quite the little sleuth! Do you know the Rangeley Lakes in Maine?"

I nodded.

"In the last decade of his life, Church purchased a compound there for the summers. Investor friends often invite me to their place in Maine, a very rustic collection of cabins and a lodge, on an island quite near to where Church's place was. We hike, we watch the birds, we discuss deals, we drink great amounts of excellent wine.

"One afternoon, after a very salubrious lunch prepared by my host's formidable Hungarian cook, we took the runabout across the lake into town to pick up the newspapers and came upon an auction next to the little general store.

"In high good spirits, we strolled inside to see what was being offered. On a dare, I bid for what everyone considered a rather lurid portrait of a beautiful, bare-breasted woman. No one else was interested and so it was mine for a few dollars. We staggered out and returned to our lodge. Only when the painting arrived at my office did I realize it was a serious work. I took it to a private dealer who authenticated the Church signature on the reverse."

"Why make up a story about the provenance?" I asked.

"Forgive an old man his need to intrigue. The truth is so often dull I feel obliged to embellish. I suppose I feel guilty about acquiring it for nothing. Besides, what difference does it make, Lindsey? The important thing is that the portrait is real and that I have now donated it to Olana for all to enjoy."

♦♦♦♦♦

INTERVIEWS ABOUT
THE UNFORTUNATE EVENING

Paul wanted me along the next day when he went to talk to Morris and Elizabeth Nelson, the couple donating the Jasper Cropsey to Olana. He said I'd take the edge off the visit and get them to relax and talk. The Nelsons live just outside of Germantown in a rambling old farmhouse overlooking a lake surrounded by willows. Their house is part fieldstone and part white clapboard. Beside the house there's a handsome pale gray barn that sits on four-foot stone foundations. That's Morris Nelson's studio. He is a stay-at-home dad who's a painter. Elizabeth Nelson runs her own PR firm in New York.

Husband and wife met us at the door and were obviously a little nervous. A visit from the sheriff does seem to make peoples' neurons fire at will. As they hung our coats on hooks in the hall both Nelsons blurted out, "Is this about the murder?"

Paul nodded. "Lindsey is helping me interview several people who were at the Olana Christmas Party. Sometimes people recall things that seemed irrelevant at the time but may prove useful in the overall context of our investigation."

"Right!" they said and took us into their library cum family room where we sat across from the fire and could see the pond through a series of good-looking three-over-one windows between well-raked dormers. Good architect, I thought. The room was informally done with big chintz couches and chairs and built-in bookcases and cabinets on three walls. I wondered if the abstracts hanging on the walls were Morris's work. Elizabeth returned with a tray of coffee and a plate of brownies. Get thee behind me, Satan, I thought, but tore off half a brownie anyway.

Morris began. "We're happy to help. What do you want to know?"

Paul said, "Why don't you tell us what you remember about that night?"

Elizabeth began. "We came early; I think we may have been the first to arrive. We gave our names to a woman at the door who checked us off the guest list. Bill van der Wyck was supposed to meet us to discuss a Cropsey we wanted to donate to the house."

"What time was that?"

"A little after five I'd say. Anyway, we were to meet van der Wyck and asked one of the docents where he was. They sent someone to look for him. He appeared in a few minutes and took us into Church's studio at the far end of the house to discuss the painting."

I asked, "Do you know where he'd been?"

"He said he'd been helping one of the groundsmen return a ladder to the carriage house."

Paul and I looked at each other. That could have put him at the back of the house at the same time Sheila had been outside.

"How long did you discuss the Cropsey?" Paul asked.

"Not long. Maybe fifteen minutes. We had already sent him a scan of the painting so he knew the work. Bill explained Olana already has a better Cropsey and suggested we sell ours and just hand over the money instead."

My eyebrows must have moved a bit because he laughed and added, "Wait! I don't mean he put it quite that way! We certainly weren't offended.

We hadn't chosen the painting---my great aunt left it to me. It has no sentimental value. We just want to support Olana. Bill wants to expand their support of young painters and doctoral students of the period."

He gestured out the window toward the barn.

"Luckily I can afford to paint. But not everyone has that luxury."

Next we went to see Dr. Charles Klyce who chairs Olana's board and who, like the Nelsons, was taking time off during the holidays. Dr. Klyce is a sports medicine surgeon who makes sure the Giants are battle-worthy during the season. He lives in a 1920s brick Georgian on top of a hill just north of Red Hook. His housekeeper greeted us at the door and led us to Dr. Klyce's den where he had a beautiful Parker over-and-under gun out on a table and was reaming the barrels with bluing. Several other shotguns were in glass cabinets on the walls. The lamps had bird dogs and double-barrels holding up the shades. The room was paneled in a dark amber pine. Well-used leather chairs sat around a couch upholstered in chocolate hopsack. There were several paintings of Irish and English setters on point and covies of birds flying up from the fields. I noticed volumes of Nash Buckingham in the bookshelves. Several tables held vases of fresh flowers. Klyce was wearing a red plaid flannel shirt with a white polo shirt underneath, dark green corduroy trousers, and moccasins.

"Hey there!" he called when we walked in. "How about some coffee? Or a glass of something?"

"Coffee'd be great," Paul and I answered.

"Thanks, Mildred." The maid nodded and left as Dr. Klyce came over to shake hands with both of us.

"My wife is taking forever at the grocery store, but from what you said on the phone, you just want to talk to me, is that right?"

Paul answered, "For the most part."

"What a gorgeous gun!" I said, walking over to the Parker.

"Where do you hunt birds up here?" Paul asked. "Mashomack?" That's a club over in Pine Plains that releases pheasants a couple of times a year.

"No, I'm a quail man. Sometimes doves. I have a buddy down in Georgia who hunts. His family has an enormous plantation, right at 20,000 acres. When he and I were in med school at Emory, we hunted there. I go down four times during the season. Twice in January, twice in February. Great bobwhite country. His family keeps good dogs. All the fireplaces are laid with Georgia fatwood. Lots of people in white jackets looking after us. It's a nice, old-fashioned trip."

He turned to Paul. "You hunt?" he asked.

"Never have. Mostly deer and turkey up here and I haven't got the patience for either."

"What about you?" He turned to me. "You're the one panting over this Parker gun! Come out back and try it!"

"Not I!" I laughed. "I've shot 12 gauge but I'm better off with a .410 or twenty. Twelve's too rough for me."

"You hunt birds?"

"I used to but it's been so long since I picked up a gun I probably couldn't hit a Hummer much less a quail."

Klyce chuckled. "Come spring, you'll come over and be my guest at this little place nearby that runs sporting clays. Ever shot those?"

"I have. I enjoy that." Sporting clays are sometime called 'golf with a shotgun.' You walk a path and clay pigeons are released periodically, some on the fly like birds and some rolling across the ground to represent a rabbit on the run.

Klyce nodded. "Then that's what we'll do. My wife Harriet's got two .410s and you can use hers." He waved his arm to us and said, "Come on over here and sit down. You getting anywhere on the murder? That's what you're here about, right? Here comes Mildred with our coffee."

Mildred set down a tray of coffee and a plate of Christmas cookies. Satan was already behind me so I leaned over and had a fruitcake bar with a date on top.

"So what's on your mind?"

Paul looked at me. I opened with, "Tell us about the last board meeting."

Dr. Klyce cradled his coffee cup, sat back in his chair, and crossed his legs. "I'll speak frankly. It was a damned brouhaha. Usually those meetings are dull as owl droppings but the last one got very rancorous. Lot of tempers flaring. I wouldn't be surprised if a few people stopped speaking to each other."

"Anybody actually lose it?" Paul inquired.

"Martha Lee flew completely off the handle. The executive committee had passed a by-laws change—Sheila's idea—that rotated directors off after a three-year stint. After a year, we could decide whether to bring them back or not. It's not a bad idea. Gives us a chance to bring new people along. But it hacked Martha off."

I said, "Martha had mentioned to me she was not happy about it."

"Not happy is putting it mildly. Try one of these little pecan pies. Mildred makes them from scratch, *will not* give my wife the recipe, makes Harriet furious.

"The real blow-up though was about this plan that's on the table to raise $30 million and build a visitors' center, and, according to some of the trustees, a B&B, an interactive media center, and God knows what else, down the hill from Olana. The disagreement goes right to the heart of what Olana's mission is supposed to be.

"Of course, we see expansion all the time with museums. In the city we live right around the corner from the Whitney. Is that expansion going to be a pain! Or look at MOMA and the Morgan. These places acquire more art, they need more space, and so they build."

"But Olana is not acquiring more art," I said.

"No, I know." Dr. Klyce sat up and put down his coffee. "Half our board believes Bigger is invariably Better. The other half, myself included, thinks we need to give it some more thought.. But Sheila believed it was the right idea and was leading the charge."

Paul brought him back. "So Martha lost her cool?"

Klyce nodded.

"It got ugly. Martha can be very haughty. She told Sheila to stick to ticket-taking and let the educated people call the shots. Of course, that remark did not endear her to our colleagues who *are* in favor of expansion." He shook his head. "It was a mess. Martha's last words were, 'I'll stop you if I have to do it myself.' I got our secretary to move for adjournment, Martha seconded it, and that was that. The next time we all saw each other was the Christmas party."

After taking leave of Dr. Klyce, we went to Olana to see Manny Feller.

He was down at Cozy Cottage, a small house on the lower property where the Church family lived during Olana's construction, retying burlap that had blown off rose bushes and stuffing new straw around the plants.

"Manny, I wish you'd come over to my house and do that," Paul said by way of greeting.

The two men shook hands and Manny and I kissed hello.

"You have a minute for some questions?" Paul asked.

"Sure do," said Manny agreeably. "Let's just step into the cottage. I'll be glad to get out of this wind."

We went inside the cottage that was heated just enough to keep the pipes from freezing and the plaster from pulling away from the lathes. The cost of heating oil these days is a scandal. We found some sunlight in the kitchen and perched on chairs in what couldn't have been more than 45°. We kept our coats on and I dug my hands more deeply into my coat pockets.

"Manny," Paul asked, "tell me again—what was wrong with the flood light the night of the Christmas party?"

"Busted in half. Wind blew off a branch that hit it, I reckon."

"What did you do after you noticed it?"

"Went down back out to the carriage house. Got a new bulb and fetched a ladder up to the house to change it."

"Were you by yourself?"

"Yep. The three other men on duty that night had give the parking lot one last shot of salt and sand and then was driving up and down the hill to see if they'd missed any icy spots.

"So, anyways, I hauled the ladder and the new bulb back up to the front door. Gave the bulb to a docent lady, Mrs. Green, Larry's wife from down at the bank, to hold so it didn't get broke. Then I went back out and set up the ladder. That darn thing gave me a time in the wind, I should say! The docent said she'd hold the ladder but just then van der Wyck came tearing out the door cussing like a sailor. He damn near ran into me and scared Mrs. Green who was standing there.

"He asked me what the hell I was doing and I told him changing a light. She told him she'd hold the ladder but Van der Wyck told her no you won't, Mrs. Green. He right away helped me put the ladder up and steadied it while I went up. He held the flashlight for me so I could see what I was doing. He calmed down while we was doing all that and apologized to Mrs. Green about his language."

"What size ladder was that, Manny?" I asked.

"It's 36 foot all the way out but I only needed about twenty feet."

"Then what happened?"

"We took down the ladder, I handed the dead half I screwed out to the docent and shone the flashlight around to find the busted shards which I gave her those. Then I went to carry it out back. Van der Wyck said he'd help me but I told him I didn't need no help on to it."

"Manny," I said, "that's kind of a big ladder to schlep around on paths that might be a tad slick. You didn't really mind Bill helping, did you?"

"Well, no, Miss Lindsey. Not really. I'm not as young as I used to be but I guess I don't like to take notice of it. I was glad to have a hand."

"So Bill helped you return it, then he went back inside."

"He did. Somebody was calling for him, said he had people there. He tore off into the house through the back door to wash his hands, he wasn't wearing no gloves. I stayed at the carriage house for a bit and washed up."

Paul thanked him and we took our leave. Manny had returned to tying burlap when Paul turned and called, "Manny! One more thing."

"Yes, Sheriff?" Manny called back as the wind whipped around us.

"Could that light have been shot out?"

"I suppose so," he answered.

"Do you keep a gun here, Manny?" Paul asked.

"No, sir. I don't. Keep 'em at home."

"Manny," I asked, "what did Sheila say when she came into the carriage house?"

"She wanted to know why I wasn't..." He stopped.

"I never said she was in the carriage house."

"But she was, wasn't she?" I asked. "She saw you with the ladder."

Manny looked away for a moment, then turned back to us.

"She told me this was my last Christmas here, enjoy it."

Paul said, "That would make *me* want to strangle her."

Manny answered, "It did make me want to. But I didn't want to get caught at it."

THE REAPPEARANCE OF
THE NEW YORK TIMES REPORTER

In the winter I move plants that won't survive outside into the dining room---and was presently tending to a dozen agapanthus and several clivia arrayed on benches below the windows. The latter had miraculously decided to bloom. Usually the clivia bloom only when I leave in winter for a Caribbean break and they can throw their orange balls in complete privacy. Every year, I reread garden books but am never able to retain what care the plants want. Water when? Don't water then? Whatever I had done or left undone had produced a glorious display and I was feeling quite proud when the phone rang.

"Lindsey?" The voice was that of Maureen Lodge, cultural reporter for the *Times*. We have known each other since the early eighties when she did a feature story on an unusually diverse estate I handled. It had several M.J. Heades and a Noel Coward watercolor of Port Maria, Jamaica I could hardly bear to sell. Maureen is terribly erudite and will inform even casual passersby of that fact in her arch Boston tones. She's a Smith education on steroids and the murder had her in overdrive.

"Yes, Maureen," I cried, setting down the fertilizer. "How marvelous to hear your voice again so soon. You should see my clivia! What's up?"

"My dear, you are in the epicenter of a whirlwind. No one can talk about anything other than Olana. What have you learned about the nude?" she inquired.

"The dead one?" I asked.

"No, the Church, my sweet. I've spoken to Van der Wyck, the curator, and I'm interviewing him for a piece on the portrait for the Sunday magazine. 'The Naughty Nude from the Lurid Landscapist.' It's as sensational a story as we'll get unless Picasso turns out to be a posthumous pedophile. And I clearly already know more about it than you do. Which I am prepared to discuss, given an early lunch."

"I'd love to hear," I said. "How can we arrange that?"

"You can start by collecting me. I'm at the train station."

We settled ourselves at the new Tuscan restaurant on lower Warren. Maureen rearranged her boa around her shoulders, ordered a Sancerre, reminded me it was Hemingway's favorite wine, and proceeded to talk the talk at full tilt. By which I mean she held forth on herself for thirty minutes, recounting battles with *her* Philistine publisher who "didn't know a cubist from a Rubik's cube," *her* managing editor "who never met a Scotch he didn't like," and the curator at Olana who had probably committed the murder and why was this fact not abundantly clear to all?

I dropped Maureen at Olana for her interview with Van der Wyck and went to learn more about Sheila's comings and goings.

A VISIT WITH THE STATIONMASTER

Thirty years ago, the Hudson station was about to fall down but the state came through with a grant and it's now been restored to its pristine red brick charm with a standing seam roof and iron fretwork on the columns. A local group has installed modern sculptures on the station's terrace. They and the surrounding trees were piled with snow as I arrived for my visit.

Billy Brenner is the stationmaster.

Other than riding a Harley to work, he is the model of a well-mannered young man in his mid-thirties with a wife and 2.3 children. His sandy brown hair is sometimes longish, sometimes crew cut. He wears gold-rimmed glasses that give him an owlish, professorial mien. His light gray Amtrak uniform and striped Amtrak tie make him appear quite the law-abiding citizen, but I detect in Billy a hint of longing for the wilder times of the Sixties, even though he was a mere zygote when my generation hit the streets. He and I have known each other for years and I've always been fond of him. When a woman is about to miss her train, he's the kind of guy who will catch keys hurled at him through tears, make the conductor stay and hold the door open, then park her car, and tuck the keys safely into his vest pocket.

I approached Billy as he was beginning his afternoon break to coincide with a lull between trains.

"Got time for coffee, young Brenner?" I asked. "I have a few points of train lore I'd like to discuss."

"If you are buying, we can talk about anything you want. Just let me close the office," he answered amiably, pulling down the frosted glass panel to close the ticket window.

We settled in at the café across the street.

"You're aware a woman was murdered at Olana last week?"

Billy replied, "Sure. It's the only thing in the paper."

"Was she a customer of yours?"

"Yeah, she went down to the city pretty often."

"Did she travel alone? Go on certain days of the week? Which train did she usually take?"

"She never went at peak. Hardly anybody here for those afternoon trains, except relatives leaving the prison. I don't remember ever seeing her traveling with anybody."

This seemed to rule out any local talent she had snuggled up to and gotten an apartment from.

"Did she carry luggage?" I asked.

"She used to carry a suitcase but she quit that several months back."

"Interesting. Thanks for being an observant soul, Billy. I'll just grab a new schedule and be on my way." I walked back to the station, cut across the waiting room, and then headed to my car. Even before I opened the door, I heard angry raised voices outside . Very rough talk. Not wanting to walk into the middle of a fight, I cracked the door slightly to see if I had a clear path to the parking lot. Peeking out I saw a swarthy-looking fellow letting out a barrage of invective, insults, and threats.

"You hire me to do a job! I come to do it but you don't want to pay me! Get this clear. You're going to pay me! You take me for a fool? Lady, I ain't no fool!"

A woman's shrill voice snapped back, "That was not the price we agreed on!"

"Sometimes things cost a little more, lady. Pay up!"

Opening the door slightly, I thought, that voice sounds familiar, and found myself staring at Martha.

"Martha!" I cried. "What's going on? Should I call the stationmaster?"

"Lindsey! Get this guy away from me!" she cried and pushed back from him.

"Don't walk away from me!" the man grabbed Martha and roughly wrenched her arm. Turning to me he said, "You can call anybody you want. She got me over here to do a job. I came and I want my money."

The train whistle cut the air and the big engine rolled around the corner slowing as it approached the station.

He shook Martha's shoulders violently again. "Pay me what you owe me! Now!"

I stepped forward and held up my phone.

"I'm calling the police."

At that, Martha cried, "No! Don't!"

Martha reached in her purse and hauled out a wad of bills held with a rubber band. She shoved it at the man.

"Here's your lousy money. Now get lost!"

I stood with Martha as the man spat out one final insult and offered a last gesture, then moved toward the train. Several yards away, Billy Brenner emerged from his office door carrying an iron stepstool. As the train stopped, a carriage door opened, the conductor emerged and swung down to help passengers. A few people exited, clutching luggage or handing bags down to the conductor and Billy. They dispersed in different directions and Martha's pal disappeared into the carriage.

I turned to Martha. "What the hell was that all about?"

"Nothing." She looked angry and exasperated.

"Like hell. What was it about?"

"I said forget about it!" Martha snapped. "Drop it."

"Do you want to tell me or do I get on the train and ask him? Your choice."

She hesitated.

"I mean it, Martha," I warned and took a step toward the tracks.

Martha barked, "Let's go sit in my car."

We got into her Volvo. Martha turned on the ignition and let the windows down so she could smoke. The train started to pull away.

She began, "Promise me if I tell you, you won't tell anybody. It was stupid. Just stupid. I didn't even go through with it."

"Go through with what?"

"That guy. I hired him to come up here to take care of Sheila."

"You hired a hit man?" I gasped.

"Not a hit man! Hell, no. Not to kill her. Just get her attention. Send her a message."

"The message being what?"

"That people in high places didn't like her ideas."

"This is about discouraging her plans at Olana?"

"I told you. I will not stand for her wasting $30 million on a crackpot idea. I thought a little warning would be enough to put her off. But we didn't go through with it!" Martha pleaded. "Nothing happened! I swear it!"

I said, "Martha, how can you say 'nothing happened.' The woman was killed! How do I know your friend didn't get carried away and do it?"

Martha protested wildly. "No! No! He just came up yesterday! There was no job for him to do! That's what we were fighting about. I didn't see why I should pay him. It's not a big deal. Anyway, I lucked out. Somebody beat me to it. She's dead."

I got out of the car. "Martha, you are insane."

Staying calm required a lot of effort as I watched Martha drive away.

When I got into my car I grabbed a notepad out of the glove compartment and jotted down a description of the man. He wasn't much taller than Martha but he was built like a football player, big through the shoulders. No neck. His head sat on his shoulders like a cannonball. He wore a fedora. Tight black sweater. Black leather jacket. Had dark sideburns running down his cheeks. Maybe middle forties.

I watched my breath condensing on the windshield and turned on the heater, then called Paul to explain what I had seen.

He said, "You stay there. I'll call you right back."

When he called he said, "I've got the conductors keeping an eye on him for a few minutes. Train 265 out of Hudson will be making an unscheduled stop in Barrytown. We'll take him off there and bring him back. Where is Martha?"

"I'll find her. Give me a few minutes."

"I'll give you half an hour to get her to surrender. Then I'm going to pick her up."

I called Eve at Olana.

"Eve, do you still have the guest list for the Christmas party?"

"I have it here somewhere. I'm looking."

"What would have happened if I had brought someone not on the list?"

"Easy. Just give us the name of your guest and pay at the door. People often bring an extra guest. We take their money and add the guests' names to our list. Okay. Here it is. What are we looking for?"

"I need to know who got added to the list for the party that night."

"You mean and killed Sheila?" she whispered.

"I don't know. Maybe. Also, do you remember who arrived first?"

"One of the first in the door was the nice couple from Germantown who are giving the Jasper Cropsey. Let's see---a few board members came very early. Every year some do to look around and make sure we haven't overlooked anything or done something gauche."

"Like what board members?"

"Dr. Klyce."

"What about Martha Lee?"

"Martha and her guest came early, too."

"Martha had a guest? What was her guest's name?"

I could hear Eve mumbling names as she flipped pages.

"Here it is. The name written beside Martha's is George Spelvin."

I snorted at that.

Eve asked, "Is something wrong?"

"No, no," I said, not wanting to reveal that a chink had appeared in Martha's armor.

Many people might not recognize that name, but I knew it, and Martha, an avid theatre buff, would know it as well. George Spelvin (or Georgette or Georgina) is a fictitious name used by actors who don't want to be credited or whose names would otherwise appear twice in a playbill when they play more than one role. In any case, there is *no such person* as George Spelvin. So who was Martha's guest?

"Do you remember this George Spelvin who was with her?"

"She said he was from out of town, a houseguest or something. I remember he was dressed in black."

"You mean black tie?"

"No, not a tux. He had a black leather jacket, black pants, and I think a black shirt."

"Do you remember anything else about him?"

"Sideburns. He had really long sideburns down below his ears."

The sun was setting over the river and George Spelvin was in the middle of a hot dog when train 265 slowly ground to a halt in Barrytown.

Two state troopers boarded, informed Mr. Spelvin he was wanted for questioning in Hudson in connection with a murder and escorted him off the train. He made a run for it but his shoes were no good in the snow and the uniforms caught him as he fell rounding the corner of the old Barrytown station. George Spelvin was bundled into a cruiser and headed back to Hudson twenty-five minutes after he had left.

Next I called Martha at home. No answer. I tried her cell and got her at the Spotty Dog, a book store on Warren Street. I rushed over and found her sipping cappuccino and thumbing through a magazine.

"Martha," I hissed, "we picked up your friend just before Rhinecliff. You lied to me! He didn't come up here yesterday. You brought him to the Olana party the night Sheila was murdered. Tell me the truth. I'm an old friend. The sheriff has given you a chance to collect your thoughts and make sense before he arrests you. I swear I hope you do. But one way or another, I think you need to call your lawyer."

Martha continued sipping. "Look, don't make a big deal out of this," she said blithely. "I admit I didn't tell you the whole thing. I thought if you knew I'd brought him to the party you'd jump to conclusions."

"Everybody is definitely jumping to conclusions, Martha, which, unfortunately, look extremely bad for you. Take a minute and call your lawyer."

"I don't need a lawyer."

"Martha, you have a lot of money and a lot of mouth but neither is going to do the trick this time. The sheriff has given me a chance to ask you to come in voluntarily. If you don't, he's going to pick you up."

♦ ♦ ♦ ♦ ♦

Eventually, Martha agreed that walking in under her own steam would look better than being arrested and we entered Paul's office just as Mr. Spelvin was arriving. Paul parked Martha in one room and Spelvin in another.

Paul persuaded Mr. Spelvin to answer a few preliminary questions. When did he come up? The night of the murder. Where had he been in the meantime? Visiting relatives in the Catskills for the holidays. Produced a stub from his northbound train ticket. Paid by Visa. Real name Richie Tizio.

After questioning them separately, Paul brought Tizio into the room where Martha sat fuming under the watchful eye of a uniformed policeman.

Tizio began talking as he walked in the door.

"Here's the story, boys and girls. You got nothing. This one"---Tizio gestured at me---"sees me at the station. I'm having a few words with my friend Martha." Martha made a face.

"I ain't done nothing. I got no gun. You can't pin no murder on me. I go to the fancy party. I look around for the chick I'm supposed to talk to, she's nowhere to be seen. I figure she's a no-show. Our plan was that I'd have a little chit-chat with her during the party where she couldn't make a scene. Just a friendly talk. Tell her some people weren't too thrilled about her plans. But hey! Guys! The last time I looked, there's no law against somebody else doing your talking for you. What are lawyers and wives for?

"As you well know, officers," he continued, a study in smarmy smugness, "the woman for whom I was in search came to the party at the end of a rope. She was dead when we got there." He cackled and cocked back in his chair with a self-satisfied sneer. His foray into the snow had wrecked his lizard slip-ons. There's $59.95 down the drain.

"Threatening someone is against the law, as is hiring someone to make threats." Paul's grim look indicated he was none too pleased. We both knew the closure we hoped for was slipping away. Not that I wanted Martha to be an accomplice to murder.

"You can ask the broad who hired me." Martha glared. "She was pissed that I wanted to get paid for my trouble, plus two days' travel and expenses. How could I lean on a woman who was very coincidentally already dead? Give me a break. I didn't threaten nobody. You got no case."

Paul asked me to step into his office. He said, "We could charge them but it isn't going to stick. This twit told us when he couldn't find Sheila, he spent the bulk of the party putting the moves on one of the caterer's girls downstairs and had a date with her the next night across the river in Greenville. That's easy enough to check out."

"So what are you going to do?"

"I have no choice at this point. Let them the hell go."

I got home just in time to snipe two lots I wanted on eBay, check my email, and indulge in a smidge of Free Cell. Martha's appalling story had put me in a foul mood.

Shortly after seven, as Bennett was laying a fire in the living room and I was filling the ice bucket, Maureen flounced in, sat down, and inquired about the evening's recipe.

"Sidecars, ladies?" Bennett suggested.

Maureen nodded enthusiastically and Bennett began the painstaking 1½ parts to ½ part to 6 parts calculations.

Serving us, he murmured to me that dinner was in the warming oven and withdrew, leaving us to our girl talk and a proper catch-up. Mother's glasses duly rimmed in sugar and safely in hand, we toasted the Ochs and Sulzberger families and then got to the point.

"While you have been spritzing plants and schmoozing doormen, I have solved the murder, dearie."

Maureen's self-satisfied smile shone brightly. Maureen's mood was 180° away from mine but I couldn't say anything. I let the sidecar do its work and kept smiling.

"How terribly efficient, darling!" I beamed. "If only you could run a household, you'd make some lucky prosecutor a wonderful wife. Who done the deed?"

"A child of four could tell you it was the curator, Van der Wyck."

"William? Why do you still think it was Van der Wyck?"

"Here's this scholar, fresh out of Chicago and Yale. He gets a post at a dusty Victorian pile in the middle of nowhere---yes, dear, I know it's an historic area if you don't mind driving past trailer parks on your way home, seeing fat women in pink hair curlers on the main drag, or having only cheddar, cheddar, and Swiss in the cheese department."

"It isn't that way any more," I protested. "We have lots of nice cheeses now."

"Whatever, you get my point. It's not as though he landed a slot at the Gardner or the Getty or the Met. He's in the sticks, curating a dozen paintings no bigger than placemats, most of which are studies. When he tells people where he works, he has to spell it and they still don't know.

"Then, suddenly, the place gets hot. Instead of preaching the *pleine aire* gospel to a bunch of yahoos, he's rubbing shoulders with the haves, he's got a budget to hire other curators, he's invited to lecture, to submit monographs, he's a contender, he's arrived. All brought about by this blonde.

"Initially he is thrilled, but then! Oh my! How she monopolizes the spotlight! People start talking to her, not him. She's the one taking lunches, hosting cocktail parties. Scholarship begins to play second fiddle to marketing. He's stuck up here while she's swanning about the Upper East Side.

"Darling, he makes no bones about it---he loathed the woman! I'm sure he killed her. She was horning in on his cornucopia."

"Let me take a moment to call the Metaphor Police. Let's set the corpse aside for a minute, Maureen," I said, topping off our glasses.

"What did Van der Wyck say about the portrait? Who's the woman?"

"He's as baffled as the rest of you. But he pointed out what could be a clue. She's wearing a signet ring. With a monogram. VK.

"The peculiar thing is that Van der Wyck cannot seem to get the straight story on the provenance of the painting. Apparently Wrangel is vague or downright obfuscatory. Tells a different story every time Van der Wyck talks to him. First he said he found it in an antiques store in Hudson. The next tale had it in some auction in Maine. Next he was nosing around a shop off Portabello Road, he can't recall. Or he might have found it on a Peru trip when he went to see Machu Pichu. Van der Wyck is baffled."

"Yes, I've gotten much the same litany. Perhaps it isn't a Church at all?" I mused.

Maureen shook her head. "No, that is the one certainty about the painting. Brush strokes, palette, canvas preparation, signature, everything is legit. No doubt whatsoever on that part. The question is which, if any, of these is the true story."

"And who is the woman?"

"We'll probably never know. By the way, Van der Wyck was explaining of the origins of the surname Church. Are you aware it was originally given to foundlings who'd been dropped off in a basket on the parish steps? With murky origins like that, how can we really be certain what the artist was up to?"

"Surname aside, we've always understood the man was a pillar of rectitude."

"That may be, most of the time. But there remains the painting of a nude."

"I can tell you the antique store in Hudson story is definitely a line," I said as I headed in to get dinner out of the oven.

Maureen hurried after me. "How do you know?"

"Maureen, hand me that pot holder. I spoke to the owner. No possibility. Just bring in the salad and we're all set." We went into the dining room, I lit the candles and we sat down to a scrumptious beef bourguignon Bennett had made that morning and a Chateau Pesquie Côtes de Ventoux which Maureen pronounced 'amusing.'"

"So the antique store was a canard. Interesting. I've got to find out where it came from. The painting had to have been somewhere in the hundred years since Church painted it."

"Last night at Huxley's, Wrangel fed me that story about finding it at an auction in Maine. I wonder if that's the truth."

"Oooooh," Maureen cooed. "Van der Wyck told me Church bought a place in Maine, up near the Rangeley lakes. Moldywicket. Something like that."

"Millinocket."

"That's it. Maybe the Maine auction is the true story. How do we run that to ground?"

"We need a list of auctioneers."

Maureen agreed. I put that at the top of my to-do list in the morning.

As we toddled off to bed, Maureen asked, in the way only an old friend would, "Had you had children, dear---what would you have had?"

"Twin girls, as always," I replied.

"And their names?"

" 'Uscita and Terminale,' I think," and kissed her forehead lightly.

MAINE AUCTIONEERS

The next morning, after sending Maureen off to town to soak up local color for her article, I went to the website for Maine auctioneers and got the names of the ones closest to the Rangeley Lakes.

My first conversation was with one Fletcher Watson who used to do auctions there but dealt only in land and farming equipment.

Then I spoke to a Finster McGrath who had retired from auctioneering and now had a bait shop and repaired chain saws. He told me to call Pru Tyler who mostly worked Down East but ran a couple of auctions each year over Rangeley way.

Pru Tyler's office in Eastport consisted of a machine which directed my call to a Boca Raton number. Mr. Tyler took my call as he was coming in from a morning round of golf. His Maine accent made me want to fly up to Blue Hill and order steamers.

"Yes, I run auctions in the Rangeley area. Do it twice a yeah, once in spring, then in summah. Always get a good crowd. What kind of boat did you say you were looking foah?"

"Actually, I wouldn't mind an old cat boat," I answered, indulging a favorite E.B. White fantasy.

"They're pretty deah just now, young lady. Not many moah being made, everyone's gone to powah lately. I have a Chris Craft, 1930. Beauty.

Got a Scripps V-12. Let you have it for a hundred. Worth a hundred and a half, easy. Needs some vahnish heah and theah."

"Mr. Tyler, do you keep a record of who bought what at your auctions?"

"Hell, yes, we keep records. Are you with the tax people? Who'd you say you were again?"

"Sir, I'm trying to establish the provenance of a painting I understand was bought in the last few years at one of your Winnisocket auctions."

"Millinocket!" barked Mr. Tyler.

"Yes, sorry, right. Millinocket," I stammered.

"Mr. Tyler, I'd be grateful if you could check your records and give me descriptions of oil paintings you've sold. Portraits of women. Just from the last few seasons.

"Oil paintings?! Hell, I don't need to check any records. We don't sell oil paintings! We don't sell any kind of paintings! We auction boats and lobstah equipment. What evah made you think we sold paintings?"

"Do any auctioneers up there sell art?"

"Not a soul, deah. Aht comes out of estates, and people with estates to liquidate go to Portland or Bah Hahbah or Penobscot.

"Millinocket is the boonies, young lady. No ahtwork evah lodged with auctioneers, not up theah. No paintings, no portraits, no buyers.

"Think about that Chris Craft."

A CLOSER LOOK AT THE PAINTING
AND SHEILA'S OFFICE

I drove up the hill to Olana.

The painting remained in the front hall, where it had been the night of the party. In the room's dusky light, I turned on the spotlight focused to bathe the portrait. I walked over to the painting, stopping several feet away, then moving closer until I was only a foot or so from her face.

The woman was very beautiful. There was something about her smile. Was it rueful? Ironic? Yes, but also knowing and filled with unmistakable pride. There was something courageous about her. The VK monogram on the ring she wore was faint but had been painted in distinctly, as if a special detail included to make a point.

But what point? Who was she? Church had never painted portraits, and yet this spoke of an intimacy, a closeness with a friend or client unknown to curators. Was there a hidden chapter in the great man's life?

After several moments, I turned away. I walked downstairs and sat alone in Sheila's office hoping to find something to pull all the pieces together---or to point to some reason for the murder.

Wandering over to the bookcase, I pulled out her copy of the Social Register. I thumbed through the Foundation Directory and glanced through several annual reports. I sat down, put my feet up on the desk, and began to leaf through the Hudson High School yearbook that had been locked in her desk. I tried to pick out a relative of Sheila's or Ted's. A rag tag bunch of kids in 1954. Boys all had crew cuts, no ducktails yet.

I could barely remember 1954. Childhood. Still planning to conquer the world from my tree house. Elvis was just appearing on the horizon, along with Bill Haley and the Comets, Fats Domino and Jerry Lee, harbingers of the revolution. 1954 was the year of Brown vs. Board of Education, when the public schools began their descent to hell in a hand basket. Eisenhower and Nixon in the White House. The great calm before the great storm. Hudson had been cleaned up a only few years before, when the houses of prostitution were closed and louche Diamond Street became noble Columbia.

The black and white photographs showed that post-war prosperity had not reached Hudson in 1954. These kids' fathers worked on farms or in the flour mill or cement plant. Their mothers worked in the pocketbook factory or made shirtwaist dresses. The kids' clothes came out of Sears catalogues or were made at home.

The photographs reminded me of how dreary my friends and I looked in the same sorts of pictures Bing had taken long ago.

The awkward 'candid' shots. Girls in simple skirts and blouses, boys in dungarees. The pale basketball team. The honor society in which everyone looked unintelligent or bored. The pathetic costumes for their senior play, *Our Town.*

Would they have performed that had they known Thornton Wilder liked boys?

As I have often wondered what happened to one or another of my school friends, I wondered what had happened to all these kids.

Were they still in Hudson, working at the hardware stores, Price Chopper or Wal-Mart?

How many were driving tractors, raising corn, apples, cows? How many got away, went to college?

I thought of Paul. He began here.

By all accounts enjoyed his youth.

Paul, the fiendishly clever one, who bought three senior rings, making his social life spectacularly successful.

He escaped, saw the world, now was back.

What did it all mean?

Where were all these young boys and girls now? They were middle-aged men and women.

No, I corrected myself. They were just past the shank of youth.

THE CATERER

The next day, as snow continued sifting down from leaden, dour skies, I sat at the dining room table having a late coffee, opening mail, paying bills, writing thank you notes and wishing I was in Boca Raton. I've never visited Boca but I hear it's nice. Morocco still sounded nice, too.

I immediately reproached myself for such wicked daydreams--- it was far too early in the winter for cabin fever. It occurred to me to go into town and scare up some hot chocolate and a new book. Or maybe drive over to the Berkshires and have lunch at Wheatleigh. The violence with Martha had shaken me. I needed to be away from the shadow of Olana.

Brightened by the prospect of getting the hell out of Dodge, I grabbed the phone to ring up Bennett and ask if he fancied an excursion to Massachusetts when Paul's face appeared at the back door. I waved him in.

Paul poured himself a cup of coffee and joined me at the dining room table. As he talked, my bright mood of escape vanished.

"The Richie Tizio-Martha Lee connection has struck a chord with me. There's something too neat, too pat about the way it ended. I've called the city and done some research on the guy. His sheet shows he's more than just a punk. I'm going across the river and do some interviewing. Want to come along?" he asked.

"I thought we ran that to ground," I said. Staring out at the snow, I saw three cardinalshaving a marvelous time on the feeder. Free as birds.

"What more is there to know?"

"I have a hunch there are plenty of things we don't know yet. Tell me about your friend Martha."

"Not a lot to tell. Filthy rich, volatile personality. Does some writing. Has too much money to develop much of a work ethic. Is overly dramatic. Easily bored. Likes to feel that she can walk on the wild side, I suppose. What's your analysis?" I asked, hoping he didn't have one.

"To begin with, she's on the wrong side of the river."

It's ridiculous, but Columbia County old timers disdain folks who live across the river. On the Rip Van Winkle bridge, there is a one-way toll going east. Headed home one day from lunch in Catskill, Paul dropped our coins into the basket and asked, "Do you know the difference between Columbia County and Green County? You can go to Green County for free but you have to pay to get into Columbia County."

"So she lives on the west bank of the river," I said. "Big deal. Not everyone can live over here in God's country."

"Coincidentally," he replied, polishing his glasses with his handkerchief, "several people on the periphery of this mess are from across the river. Our boy Tizio for one. You know, Lindsey, crooks are not new to the Catskills. Organized crime has been up in those mountains since Prohibition. Legs Diamond ran a big operation up here. It's not the major leagues now, not even triple-A ball, but it *is* the mob.

"And also present at the murder scene, we have the caterer. And where was the caterer from?"

I replied, "Across the river."

Paul nodded.

"His base of operations is a hotel called Brother Alfredo's up past Palenville in the mountains. It's a glitzy place where the guys with big gold chains and the gals with big hair do karaoke and listen to crooners from the 1950s.

"Turns out our caterer, one Anthony Schwartz, and Tizio grew up together in the Catskills and spent summers working at boarding houses. Both have records for assault. So? Like to take a ride?"

This was grim news. "I see. Better not. I have to finish all this mail, plus I have clients coming over. I've already postponed our meeting twice."

Then I threw a ballpoint pen across the room.

"Paul, you *cannot* honestly believe that Martha has lost her mind and done anything so seriously stupid! You're chasing a wild idea because we don't have anything else yet. Martha has a nice life. She's not going to risk everything because someone annoyed her! She has a lot to protect."

"Lindsey, look at the facts. Martha definitely hired someone to, quote, 'lean on Sheila.'"

"Yes, you have a point," I agreed, "and that was stupid. But Tizio was not a killer, he was a half-assed punk hired to frighten Sheila. This is going nowhere." I realized I was trying to talk him out of going.

Paul nodded. He stood up. "I'm sure you're right but I'm going to check it out. The caterer is overdue for a chat anyhow. I'll stop by when I get back." And he left.

I thought about what Huxley had said. Pollyanna.

It was close to seven when Paul returned. He came in the kitchen door and found me washing dill. He looked angry.

"What can I get you?" I asked.

"Bourbon."

This was not a good sign. Paul rarely touches liquor. He walked over to a window and stared out at the snow which was turning to freezing rain. Ice was starting to coat the tree limbs.

I got his George Dickel and took it over to him where he stood, then took my own glass of rum and water and sat down in one of the wing chairs in front of the fireplace, waiting for him to take a seat.

Paul came over and stood in front of the fire, sipping, saying nothing. His silence made me tense.

"So what did you learn?" I finally asked, trying to sound casual.

He answered me with his question from the morning.

"Tell me about your friend Martha."

"I've done that already."

"Does she have any hobbies? What does she like to do for recreation?"

"Years ago, when she was thinner, she played a mean game of tennis. She still follows it, usually goes to Wimbledon, the U.S. Open. Likes the theatre. Sees everything on and off Broadway. What does this have to do with anything?"

I knew I sounded testy.

"What is emerging is that I know a hell of a lot more about your friend Martha than you do."

"Like what?"

"Did you know she is a serious stakes poker player?"

"Poker?" I asked, incredulous.

He nodded.

I shrugged.

"Lots of people play poker. Very hot these days. It's the new bridge."

"She plays every week. Regular game across the river."

"Where across the river?" I asked.

"At Brother Alfredo's, the hotel where the caterer is based. Yep. She's right in there with the guys. That's where she met her buddy Mr. Tizio."

"I thought he was from New York City?"

"That's what he said and that's what he'd like to think. In fact, he's the bag man for a band of merry men that's a local branch of one of the New Jersey families. He goes back and forth with the percentage that goes into the big treasury."

"When did Martha start playing poker there?" I felt like we were talking about someone I didn't know.

"Tony Schwartz, who was the caterer that night, may I remind you, says back in the summer Martha stopped in for lunch. Met him and Tizio at the bar. They start talking, he and Tizio are dropping names, acting suave. She came right out and asked if they were the mob, like they're going to tell her. So Tizio says, like he's an extra in Goodfellas, 'Just let me know if you ever need any help.' "

Paul continued. "They're both disgusting. These are baby wiseguys who would pee in their pants if they ever actually met one of the big boys. They've spent too damn much time watching the Sopranos.

"Martha asks what they do when they're not being hoods, and he says, 'We play a little poker.' He tells her there's a hush-hush game every Tuesday night. Would she like to play, stay over at the hotel as their guest? Well, of course, she wants to get in the game. Clearly she's green as a gourd about all this and obviously loaded. Candy from a baby.

"So it's a Tuesday night and their little gambling operation in the back room is cranking away. Some guy loses a big pot and says he's a little short. Asks to put in a chit. So they start to rough him up, it spills out into the dining room, and some tourist calls the cops. When the sheriff shows up, everything is fine, nobody files a complaint. The guy goes to the hospital, has his head wired back together, and the show goes on. Martha's at the table that night."

"Just because she saw a fight doesn't make her a killer. Martha has a weakness for the seamier side of life. I suppose she thinks it's material for one of her plays."

"Lindsey, that's where she got the idea."

"What idea?"

"You heard me. Talk about an easy mark! Tons of dough and a brain no bigger than a $5 chip. She thinks she's hanging out with the Corleones. Naturally she talked to them about her little problem with Sheila."

At times like these, I remember there's a big difference between my background and Paul's. I helped him out with some smuggling cases but essentially I'm an art historian who has some puzzle-solving ability.

Paul is a cop. A damn good cop. With insights into human nature that I simply don't have. Yes, I can spot a pretender or a sycophant, but as Huxley pointed out, I *am* a Pollyanna. I believe--I *want* to believe---the best about people. I close my eyes to the dark side of human nature and live in a bubble. I like my bubble.

Paul continued. "Martha is in the game that night and sees some schmo get a taste of discipline. Aha! She thinks of Sheila! She thinks, good idea! None of this can be traced to her. All cash.

"Martha's on the trustee committee for the party. Martha knew the layout of the house. Have you read the damned minutes of the board meetings? I have. Martha *insisted* on the caterer, then sat in when they came over to meet with Sheila and Eve."

I shuddered. It was too much to ignore.

Paul went on. "This is the way it happened. The caterer arrives with his vans. Sheila meets them outside to check them in and show them where she wants things put. They hauled her into one of the vans, strangled her, then put the body on one of their trolleys with a tablecloth over it and wheeled it in along with the plates, glasses, and other stuff. They already had the rope around her neck. Stringing her up, then pulling the drapery around her would have taken less than a minute."

"But there were people everywhere."

Paul got up, threw a log on the fire. He took my glass, then went to the bar and freshened both our drinks.

"Yeah, I know the timing was tricky. But do you know the one thing that makes me right about this?" he asked, handing me my rum.

"Do you remember seeing a dead woman hanging in front of you? Someone killed her. And who better to manage tight timing than a bunch of pros. Not a first-rate bunch of thugs, I'll grant you, but everybody gets lucky once in a while. I'm arresting them. I've called Judge Kramer to get the warrants and I'm bringing them in tomorrow. Along with Martha."

A cold, empty feeling settled in the pit of my stomach.

"Paul, you only have circumstantial evidence. You don't really have any proof."

"No, dear, that's not quite correct. I do have proof. I am charging her, Lindsey. And *you* are going to be my star witness.

"You saw the payoff."

MARTHA IN JAIL

The warrants were signed. Martha, Richie Tizio, and Tony Schwartz were taken into custody the next morning.

This time Martha did call her lawyer.

Martha's hearing found me sitting in the city courtroom along with the usual Hudson suspects. The city courtroom, which is in one half of the police station on Warren Street, is about 30 by 60 feet. A bookcase is filled with maroon and gold volumes of the New York State Code Annotated. Walls are paneled in brown plastic wood. An aisle runs down the center of the room to the bench and the audience sits in folding chairs on either side.

Normally this hearing, a Supreme Court matter, would be in the courthouse but Hudson only has two courtrooms and both were in use that day. So, in addition to being charged with murder, Martha had the ignominy of being arraigned in front of people who had been hauled in for DWI, public lewdness, and non-payment of child support.

Paul sat in front behind the district attorney's table. Martha's attorney had come up from the city and was standing locked in conversation with the DA.

Martha was escorted in by a uniformed matron . She was wearing what appeared to be a gray wool shroud from Dior's 1953 sack collection.

Her dark hair hung lankly and I could see gray roots at the part. A sorry spectacle.

The DA made the extremely valid case that bail should be denied because there was a risk Martha would bolt and never be around to stand trial.

Martha's lawyer pointed out she had every reason to clear her good name and no intention of spending the rest of her life as a fugitive. Her lawyer appealed to the judge to set bail at $50,000 and give Martha a GPS ankle bracelet to locate her 24/7.

The DA turned to Paul and said, "Do we have those?"

Paul scowled and said, "Hell, no! We don't have ankle bracelets."

Martha's lawyer spoke up again. "If it please the court, we have obtained an ankle bracelet and we will pay for the GPS monitoring."

Paul scowled again and repeated, "I said no! An ankle bracelet won't keep her from running. She needs to stay in jail."

And so it devolved that Martha Lee, Teflon and light switch heiress, was remanded to the jail in the city of Hudson, County of Columbia, in the State of New York to await trial.

Talk about torn! I am genuinely fond of Martha---yet I am also the star witness for the prosecution! I was not only engulfed by the moral obligation to care for those who are suffering, who are in need, who are in the slammer---but by despicable, venal thoughts about my appearance on the stand. How to resolve this dilemma?

I immediately called Huxley.

Hux set a land speed record arriving and brought the pug with him which meant he intended to stay over. He emerged from his Range Rover and I hurried down the walk to collect him and his overnight bag. Achilles shot by us to the bird feeder and routed two cardinals.

We got inside and Huxley immediately began.

"I cannot believe Martha has been arrested!? What can we do? Have you talked to her?!"

"I can't talk to her. I'm the main witness".

"You're the what!???"

Huxley can achieve the soprano range when truly startled.

I had told him nothing about the progress of the case and what had transpired to date but at this point I saw no reason to hold anything back.

"Get in here!" Huxley bellowed at the pug who raced through the mud room and tore off upstairs into God knows where.

Huxley hurled his cape onto a wooden bench in the mudroom, sat down and yanked off his boots and said, "I worry that you have not been entirely forthcoming with me. I will overlook this lamentable lapse and wait," his voice growing louder, "for you to tell me EVERYTHING!"

I put out a bowl of water and a carrot for Achilles then guided Huxley into the living room.

"What shall we have?"

Huxley answered, "Clearly the time has come for us to throw caution to the winds---I'll have a Cosmopolitan."

Huxley was dressed like a refugee from Barney's warehouse sale. He sported a dark rust wool Dolce et Gabbana tunic and a pair of Army trousers he had kept after his landing at Omaha on D-Day. The costume was topped off by a muted mustard and gray plaid scarf.

He had on a baseball cap that said 'Don't!' and took it off, smoothing the gray stubble on his head.

Drink in hand, and the fire coaxed back to life---there is so much more work in winter than in summer, don't you find?---Huxley demanded, "Where is she now?"

"She's at the county jail."

"Explain it to me! I need details! Details!"

"Martha has been arrested along with the caterer and a thug she hired to either lean on Sheila or kill her depending on whether you believe Martha's story or the sheriff's intuition. The thug and caterer are people from across the river. They're in the Mafia."

"Martha has friends in the Mob? This is a disaster! What do her lawyers say?"

"Who the hell knows what they say? Our problem is that I saw Martha paying the man off! What am I to do?! I'm forced to testify against her!"

Huxley waited until I sank into the chair opposite him, lifted his glass and mused.

"Well, this is a sordid tale. It'll take months before the thing actually comes to trial. Probably summer. It promises to be traumatic.

"Why don't you wear that teal Nina Ricci thing?"

RETURN PHONE CALL FROM BING

Shortly after eight the next morning, Huxley, Bennett and I were standing on the porch with binoculars looking at the eagle who sits in the top of a dead locust every morning. I think the bird has his coffee, then pops over to gaze down at the river and see what might be available for breakfast. He and his wife had babies last spring and sometimes all four eagles sit in the tree together.

Bennett and Huxley withdrew to the living room to read the paper and listen to Dvorak, then had a spirited backgammon tournament while discussing a rehearsal of the Joan Crawford they had sat in on. I gathered it was coming along nicely but needed better wigs and some new lyrics.

I sat in the office catching up on correspondence and looking online for a highboy, a dining table, and a sideboard for a client whose house needed everything from a weathervane to a wine cellar.

At eleven, the two men took themselves down to Northwind Farm down by Kerley's Corners in Tivoli to pick up a fresh hen. When they returned, Bennett began making a coq au vin. In due course, he opened a Château Bel Air Haut Medoc 1995. Our neighbor up the hill's family started Sherry-Lehman and when I learned Bel Air was their house red, I immediately followed suit.

As the hour of our late luncheon approached, I went to find Huxley who lay reading on a chaise on the balcony.

I called up to him, "Luncheon is shortly served, milord."

Hux arose and stood at the railing staring down at me. "I'm not coming down. I have no appetite."

The house was redolent with the aromas of the chicken, the bacon, and Bennett's sauce, and I couldn't fathom his reluctance.

"Mais il faut, Milord!" I called in mock exasperation. "Master Smythe, you wash your little paws and come down here this minute."

"OoooooooHhhh!" Huxley wailed. "How can you even think of eating when poor Martha Lee is incarcerated? Yes, *shackled* this very moment, deprived of even the *simplest* creature comforts! The indignity! The ignominy! How can I even contemplate coq au vin....and what else??" He paused.

"We've got a little pear and Roquefort over mâche and a cherry clafoutis. But if you are mired in a slough of despond, don't bother coming down! Bennett!" I called out. "Send Mr. Smythe's portion to the women's house of detention!"

Huxley roared, "Not so fast, my insolent sous chef!" and headed for the stairs. Hux strolled into the kitchen and Bennett announced, "I say, Smythe. Let's break a few rules today, shall we?"

"As in Marquess of Queensbury, one hopes?" asked Huxley with a stage leer.

"Actually, to be more precise, I'm suggesting that with our hostess's permission we flout convention!"

"I do hope you're not suggesting we carry on badly," frowned Huxley.

"Hardly, sir. I'm suggesting we aperitif out of season. I have a fresh pine, a mango, a blood orange and two Meyer's lemons and they would seem appropriate to concoct a rum punch, even though we are in the dead of winter."

"Juice at will!" replied Huxley and walked in to help me finish setting the table.

As we sat sipping before lunch, each of us fantasizing that we were on some Port Antonio veranda or pink sand beach, Bennett asked, "Are you both convinced that Martha is guilty as charged?"

I answered, "Martha would rather lie than drink coffee. It is impossible to know when she is telling the truth and, unfortunately, this is one of the few times in her life when it matters. She has a terribly overactive imagination and a fascination with the sleazier side of our fellow man. I don't know that she asked to have Sheila killed. However, she clearly hired the goon, at the least, to discourage Sheila and it is entirely possible things got out of hand."

Huxley said, "On the other hand, it is also entirely possible that Martha had every intention of bumping her off and at this point in the game has completely rationalized it. I'm sure she believes Olana and the huddled masses yearning to breathe free in our historic Valley would be better off without Sheila's siphoning off an unconscionable amount of money from worthier projects. In Martha's mind, she had Sheila killed for the betterment of mankind."

Bennett swirled the drink in his glass and looked pensive. He said slowly, "I keep thinking that we are looking at the crime from one direction only. I wonder if we oughtn't try to turn the motive around."

"How do you mean?" Huxley asked.

"We feel Sheila was murdered because someone wanted to stop her expansion plans. We also know she had come into a lot of money. Suppose someone was paying her to promote the expansion, to push it through because of personal gain, then silenced her when she threatened to reveal the collusion---or pressured him for even more money."

"Hmmmmm," Huxley and I mused.

Bennett continued to ponder aloud.

"Who would stand to gain from an expansion?"

Huxley said, "The contractor, for one."

Bennett continued. "Yes, the contractor, any of the major tradesmen. But once the expansion was in place, if it proved an attraction, the greater long-term gain would be in sympathetic development nearby. Any idea who owns the land next to the proposed building site?"

I picked up the phone and called Paul.

"Save me a trip to the assessor's office," I asked. "Call in your official capacity and find out whose land abuts the state acreage where Sheila wanted to build the new museum."

Paul called back in ten minutes to say, "Dr and Mrs. Charles Klyce. He has also gotten a building permit for a fifty room hotel and ten houses. Where did this incredible insight come from?"

I said, "This one we chalk up to Bennett. Sounds like we need another talk with Dr. Klyce."

Paul said, "Oh, yes! And we need a look at his bank records. I'll get started on the subpoenas and find out if the doctor is in. I'll call you back."

"Bennett!" I cried. "You clever soul! You're onto something!"

I put the receiver down. The phone promptly rang again. Bing Morgan's voice boomed, "We've got him now!!"

"Got who?" I asked.

"Your boyfriend Wrangel. He's wanted in six states for counterfeiting and running guns to Colombia."

"Very funny, Bing. And I am Marie of Roumania. What did you learn?"

"I learned that, according to Immigration, there was no such person, no Lucius Wrangel or any Wrangel shown entering the United States any time in the forties."

"Is it possible he came in under the radar?"

"That's highly doubtful but I suppose it is possible. Lucius Wrangel only began to exist in 1958 when his Social Security number was issued. Don't know if that helps. He got it when he started at a brokerage downtown. From a data perspective, that's his maiden voyage."

I rang off and reported the news to Bennett and Huxley. I turned back to the river and pondered.

Where had Lucius Wrangel been in the intervening years?

DR. KLYCE REDUX

After lunch, Paul collected me and we drove to Germantown and pulled into Klyce's driveway.

Paul said, "I've gotten the subpoenas. The bank records should be in later today. What's our angle going to be?"

"I would go the straight route. Let's just hear what he has to say."

Mildred the maid let us in and we returned to the study where Klyce had been cleaning his guns. He stood up from his desk as we walked in and greeted us in his normal hearty fashion.

"Still working as the shadows lengthen!" he called out cheerily as he walked toward us to shake hands. "Tying up loose ends? Come on in. What can we get you?" he asked. "Coffee? Tea?"

Paul and I shook our heads. "Just a few follow-ups, doctor, if you can spare us a few moments."

"Always happy to burnish my law-abiding reputation. Unbelievable about Martha! I damn near fainted when I read about it in the paper. Mildred's sister is a women's warden in the jail and she says Martha is a mess about this. Cannot imagine how she expected to pull it off in the first place. Sit down, sit down."

I began. "In our earlier conversation, Paul and I got the distinct impression that you were against the planned expansion at Olana. Is that a fair assessment?"

"Well, let's just say I'm not sure it would be the best idea."

Paul said, "This is a really nice place. When did you buy?"

"Oh, years ago, definitely at the right time. Can you believe what's happened to real estate up here? Prices are out of this world. Still a value, of course, but not like when you could buy an entire farm for fifty thousand."

"Do you own other property?" I asked.

"We do. We bought several buildings in downtown Hudson over the years, mostly because we didn't want to see them torn down. That sounds laughable now but you surely remember the bad old days when the cement plant was in full swing, the dust settling all over down town, and the entire tax base on Warren Street was Rogerson's Hardware, Ziesenitz stationers, and the Town Fair toy store. It looked like a ghost town. Anything could have happened."

"Any other land?" Paul asked.

Klyce leaned forward and rested his arms on his knees

"Oh hell! Let's not beat around the bush, Sheriff. I gather you've learned I own the land across from Olana."

Paul nodded. "We also learned you have submitted plans for a hotel and surveyed several home sites overlooking the mountains. You never sold an easement on the view shed there?"

Over the last twenty years or so, to protect the sightlines from Olana, preservation groups have purchased view-shed easements stipulating no additional construction.

"That parcel is not in the sightlines. But one could make the case that even if it is, the building of the museum itself would nullify any view-shed claims. What's sauce for the goose, if you see my point."

"Are the other board members aware you own the land? Are they aware of your proposed development plans?"

Klyce sat back abruptly and threw his hands in the air.

"What I do as a private property owner is not the subject of Olana board meetings!" he snapped. Taking a calmer tone, he continued, "Sheriff! Lindsey! Come on! Let's not get excited about something that is quite far from being a *fait accompli*! Yes, I filed plans for proposed development. I'm only making sure I have a fallback position if indeed the expansion comes to pass. And that's a big if, especially in light of Sheila's demise."

"Why is it a big if?" I asked. "You told us the board was split on the question. And you have quite an upside if the deal goes through. Was the Olana expansion plan your idea or Sheila's---or did you work on it together?"

Klyce got up and walked over to the bar and poured himself a glass of red wine. "Sheila had the idea on her own. I sat at that board meeting when she first proposed it, listening, listening. And frankly, I was opposed to it in principle. But, as you might imagine, I was really of two minds. Who am I to say it's a bad idea? Not all development is wrong. Look at downtown Hudson! Look at Bard College! Things change!"

"When did she figure out you owned the adjacent land?" I asked.

"Little Sheila was nothing if not thorough. Every 'i' dotted kind of person. She already had all the tax maps as a part of her work on view shed easements. On the maps the property is listed in my wife's maiden name. Sheila told me it just popped out at her one day."

"What was your relationship with Sheila?" I asked.

"She was an employee," Klyce answered. His voice had become hard. "Help me understand what you're driving at here. You've already made an arrest in this case. Most people would assume you have enough evidence for a conviction. Aren't these questions beside the point?"

"What was Sheila's salary?" Paul asked.

"I don't remember exactly. Something like a hundred and a half."

"Not enough to buy a co-op in the city?"

He didn't look surprised but answered, "Where Sheila lived is none of my concern."

"Where would she have gotten the money for that kind of purchase?"

"I haven't the vaguest idea. Are you suggesting I gave it to her? Is that your theory? Because I have a building permit? That I paid her to push through a development plan so I could make a killing on the land next door? Even if I did, how would you prove it?" He smiled.

"Look at your bank records?"

"If I were doing something shady, why would I be so stupid as to leave a paper trail? Anybody heard of Cayman? The Seychelles?"

"What time did you arrive at the Christmas party?"

"I arrived at a little after five. I always come early to look things over."

"Was your wife with you?"

"No, she had a cold and didn't want to go."

"Did you see Sheila when you arrived?"

"No."

"When did you last see her?"

"I told you. At the board meeting."

Taking a wild shot, I said, "The bartender at Gotham saw you."

He glared at me.

"Look, from time to time Sheila and I met when she was in the city to discuss Olana issues. There's nothing odd about that. She was frequently in town to meet with donors or other board members. Sometimes we met over a drink. A time or two we had dinner! Imagine! Had *dinner!*"

Klyce laughed and shook his head. "Look, you may think you're on to something but you aren't. Look at the board minutes. I'm on record as opposing the expansion. As far as my owning the property, chalk it up to coincidence. You can't even prove that Sheila knew I owned it."

Paul said. "I'm going to ask you to come into my office tomorrow morning to make a statement. That will give you time to think about things and also time to get your attorney up from the city, as you see fit. Good evening, Dr. Klyce."

As we headed home, I asked, "What do you think we got?"

Paul answered, "The main thing we got? He didn't flat out deny anything."

A VISIT TO THE ARCHIVIST

Betty McKinstry, our town archivist, has lived in Hudson every moment of her 83 years but she knows so much about the area she might as well have been aboard Henry Hudson's caravelle.

I greeted her in the Hudson Historic Society's offices in what was the old Library, a limestone block building we are finally repointing and painting.

The museum reflects the town's history as a whaling port in displays of harpoons, huge flensing knives, and other whaling tack, as well as Hessian uniforms and slave bracelets, and all manner of hardware, tools, railroad and sea-faring paraphernalia from the colonial era into the early 20th century.

Cases of artifacts chronicled the sailing ships that left Hudson for the Ivory Coast, Japan, South America, and the Caribbean. Ships would be gone for a year, sometimes two. They left with pig iron, corn, and tools, and returned with indigo, bolts of cloth, rum, spices, and china. Early photographs and engravings show teeming wharves and a booming town with a population of almost 60,000.

"Betty," I began, "I need to know two things: First, where would a Hudson resident have bought a fine gold ring?   And second, does the monogram 'VK' ring any bells? Any prominent citizens in the late 19th century have those initials?"

" 'VK,' " she repeated and thought for a moment. Shaking her head, she said, "Can't say anybody comes to mind right off. I'd have to do a little research. But buying a gold ring? That's an easier one. You should ask Tiffany's."

"Tiffany's!" I cried. "Why do you think it would have come from Tiffany's?"

"It's not a sure thing, just an educated guess, a place to start. The barons of the Valley were very much Tiffany's customers. Tiffany's made their daughters' engagement rings, their households' flatware and china, even their sporting trophies.

"Tiffany's were very forward-thinking proprietors. They were the first to have fixed, non-negotiable prices on their goods and the first to sell from a catalogue. Having a personal representative call on some of their best customers is just further proof of their good business sense, wouldn't you agree?

"Several times a year the firm would dispatch clerks with cases of whatever baubles or bijoux were in favor at the time to pay visits on the firm's favored clients. The local worthies would receive the dark-suited young man with his presentation cases and velvet pouches in the privacy of their drawing rooms, inspect and select whatever pleased them for their wives, mothers, babies, brides, whoever needed a gift.

"I will say the firm keeps absolutely scrupulous records. Their archives are fascinating! I was researching the Hudson-Newburgh sailing race several years ago and Tiffany not only had the original drawings of the trophy made for the race, they were even able to give me a complete list of contestants and winners! That was 1909 and the young man who helped me said they have records going back to 1837 when the store was Tiffany & Young and was all the way downtown in the financial district."

"Betty, you are a marvel! Come with me to Fifth Avenue and let us investigate…" I caught myself, smiled, and stepped back.

"Investigate what, dear?" Betty smiled.

"You've asked me a lot of questions, but I'm afraid you haven't told me very much about what you're really interested in. Anything to do with that unfortunate woman at Olana?"

"This won't be the last of our conversations, dear," I said, helping her with her coat and slipping into mine. "I'm afraid I can't say very much just now. Let me get a little closer to the truth of the matter, and then....Oh! I almost forgot. Here are some pictures from the party that night."

I handed her several photographs from the Olana Christmas party. They had never run in the paper because of the evening's unpleasant conclusion.

Betty looked at all the pictures, then tapped on the one of Wrangel. "Who is this man? When I saw him that night, I kept thinking, he looks so familiar. Maybe he's just handsome!"

"Lucius Wrangel. He's from the city. You know him?"

"No, I don't know that name. Seems like I've seen him before. Couldn't say where, though."

"Could have been another Olana party? Friends of Hudson? Opera Ball?" I suggested. "He gets around a lot and so do you."

She shook her head. "Maybe so," she shrugged. "Or maybe I've just seen his picture in what passes for the 'society pages,' these days." She laughed. "Ah, well. It's my old mind again. Hey! You're supposed to be taking this old mind to lunch, dearie!"

And we went into town.

A VISIT TO KINDERHOOK

Route 66 is the road you take out the back side of Hudson to Kinderhook. Alas, there are no sightings of Marty Milner and George Maharis, only memories of the catchy Nelson Riddle theme song that was about another route 66 altogether. But I digress.

Here we have lovely undulating farmland flanked by the foothills of the Berkshires and the Catskills looming well west to your left. The story of Kinderhook begins in the earliest days of Dutch exploration in the New World. In 1609 when Hendrick Hudson sailed up the river which bears his name today, historians think it likely that the most northerly anchorage of the *Half Moon* was in Kinderhook waters.

The Dutch ship attracted hordes of curious Mohican children gathered to observe the strange, never-seen-before vessel, causing a whimsical Hudson to name the place 'Kinderhoeck,' Dutch for 'Children's Corner.' The name Kinderhook appears on Dutch maps as early as 1614 and is, therefore, the oldest town in New York.

Kinderhook was also the home of Martin Van Buren, his birthplace standing among other old stately mansions on the tree-lined main street. Washington Irving wrote his Rip Van Winkle tales and drafted *The Legend of Sleepy Hollow* while working as a tutor in the village. Don't forget to leave a gratuity at the end of the tour.

Turning right at the light, I drove another few miles past farmland and then came to a vast Victorian pile painted lilac, the home of the widower Ted Marks.

The house was on an enormous corner lot in a yard filled with specimen trees. One enormous hemlock must have been a hundred years old. A family of chickadees was skipping Palm Beach, wintering instead among the rose hips in the hedge. Across a rough-hewn fence bright red Russian hawthorn berries stood out against the snow. The lovely smell of wood smoke was in the crisp, cold air.

I was greeted by three golden labs who mistook me for a belated Santa bringing toys. I gathered my coat about me and headed up the brick path to the back door, caressing the dogs' muzzles to keep them at bay. Ted Marks leaned out, calling to the dogs and me, "Don't let them bother you. They're perfectly friendly. Stop it, Turk. Alice, you and Gertrude sit down. No, you are not coming in. Here," he said, taking my arm and pulling me into the back porch. "Come in quick before they think they're joining us."

The kitchen was just off the back porch with a big square pine table at its center. A bright red Aga range occupied one wall. White-painted shelves and glassed cabinets overflowed with china, old mixing bowls, glasses of every shape and size. I could smell coffee. A fire was burning in the fireplace.

"Let me have your coat. How do you take your coffee?"

"Black, please."

"Have a seat." Ted slipped on a mitt and pulled a pan out of the oven, setting it on a trivet in front of us, then brought over mugs.

"I made some crumb cake. Mother's recipe. What else is brown sugar for, do you suppose? Everybody has it, but what do they do with it?"

"Some people put it in barbecue sauces, a heathen practice. I personally use it in French toast, and that's pretty much it---oh, except for that tuna steak in the Oyster Bar cookbook. Great stove! I take it you're the cook?"

"Always have been," he said. "How do you do your French toast?" he asked.

"Eggs plus some rum, the brown sugar, then squeeze in some orange juice and grate the rind. Get it done the night before. The bread only absorbs well if it lies around over night."

"That's what I do now," he mused. "Lie around all night. Although I gather Paul has decided my alibi is holding up."

"Apparently you were the belle of the ball at the Turnpike Lodge that evening. Everyone remembers your coming out after your nap, leading the carols, excelling at darts, and imitating Wayne Newton. No, Ted, no one believes you killed your wife."

"I realize I didn't seem sad enough for Paul. What he doesn't realize is the marriage ended so long ago, I couldn't really mourn for her any more. I finished mourning years back."

I let him talk.

"I guess sometimes people just grow apart. To begin with, I got into the wrong line of work. You know, I never gave much thought to what I was doing with my life until I was in the middle of it. I'm not cut out to be a lawyer---or at least, I'm not cut out to be a lawyer the way I am here. I've hated my life for years. Drinking was the only anesthesia available. I needed something to sober me up and Sheila's death did it. To be gone so instantly. I spent years trying to fix our lives, get her to come back to me. Completely failed. That and the office are the reasons I started drinking. Couldn't see any way out."

Ted stood and walked over to the coffee pot and brought us both a touch-up. Holding his mug he began to walk around the kitchen as he talked.

"We were so in love in the beginning. Then suddenly nothing worked anymore. I didn't want to go to the parties she did, had no interest in the people she was meeting. A hell of a lot of them were so pretentious. Restoring this house has given me pleasure---and, at first, being with me, working with me, made her happy. When we got married, we worked on it every evening, did almost everything ourselves. We'd strip wallpaper or paint or hang draperies, then fall over onto the floor and make love. Then one day, bang! She didn't like this house. Couldn't stand this town. Stopped seeing our friends, never returned their calls. She kept moving away emotionally. In a matter of a year or so, the woman I married had vanished.

"At about the same time, I was getting a lot of pressure at the office to deliver two thousand hours a year. That's hard to do in a Hudson firm. The senior partners were constantly badgering me to call on companies in Albany and Poughkeepsie. They suggested I should bill more hours on the cases I had. Told me to forget about taking cases that couldn't pay full freight. Charge a fee just for taking a case before cracking a book or drafting a brief.

"All of these things started to collide about five, six, seven years ago. Same time, Sheila started going into the city a lot for receptions, dinners, always staying overnight."

"Do you think there was another man?"

"There must have been another man. Where else would she get the money? It's so obvious now. All those nights away. Where else would she have gotten a few million dollars and an apartment?"

"The sheriff and I have been over everything in her office. There's nothing that points to a killer. Have you looked through her papers?"

. He nodded. "I found a file of correspondence---just notes, mostly. Most look like thank you letters. Would you like to see those?"

"Yes, please."

I leafed through a file Ted handed me. Sheila had kept several hand-written notes from various board members, donors---- Lucius Wrangel and Honoria among them. All seemed perfectly cordial expressions of gratitude for a tour, a visit, a lunch. None seemed of any consquence. Perhaps they were simply among her souvenirs?

"May I hang onto these for a bit?" I asked.

Ted nodded.

"Have you been down to the city to look at the apartment?"

"Not yet." He grimaced.

"You're not a fan of old New York?"

"That's not true. I just haven't been there much. It is intimidating."

" 'Intimidating,' reminds me of the first time I ever came to the big city. Was I ever floored! But, like most transplants, now I can't imagine life without New York. In the early days, I wasn't comfortable being away from Manhattan for any extended length of time, like that Frank O'Hara poem where he said he couldn't even enjoy a blade of grass unless there was a subway handy. Still, after a while, maintaining perspective is only possible with a weekend house. The city's great, but getting away is important."

"What's the best thing about New York?"

I easily answered.

"The cloak of anonymity. One can be absolutely invisible, unknown. One can be or become anything. The only limits are imagination. Sounds like you might be thinking of paying us a visit?"

Ted replied, "New York has opportunities for public advocacy lawyers. I'm thinking about that. Now that I have an apartment in town, I guess I should use it. Nothing wrong with being a weekender up here."

He made a wry smile.

"Before you go, will you come for dinner at my house on Wednesday?" I asked. " It's Epiphany."

He nodded. I kissed his cheek and headed home.

DOWN THE TACONIC TO FIFTH AVENUE AND FIFTY-SEVENTH STREET

A morning drive down to the city is one of life's great pleasures. Leaving home shortly after eight o'clock, I drove the back way to Jackson Corners and the Taconic Parkway, passing through Livingston and Blue Stores.

At that hour, morning fogs still nestle in the hollows of the stark and snowy hills. In upper Dutchess, the parkway threads through picturesque, rolling farmland with long, panoramic views stretching to the mountains past old farm houses and barns. In winter, most of the trees are stark and leafless but there are also great stands of evergreens against the snow.

In lower Dutchess and Putnam counties, the Taconic follows a high, narrow ridge through wild, mountainous terrain. The deep cuts into the rugged mountainsides are braced with massive stone retaining walls. Going south, rustic wooden guardrails or low walls protect cars that might veer eighteen inches to the right from plunging over steep precipices. In places, the road's tight curves pass through narrow woodland corridors. Ancient rhododendrons overhang large rock outcroppings. Formal plantings put in sixty years ago have merged with the old forest. Stone bridges arch across the parkway occasionally. The medians are broad and hold thick copses of trees. In many places, north and south lanes are at different elevations and one has the sense of driving on an isolated country lane.

The Taconic is an unforgiving road, but if you enjoy driving, as I do, the curves and cornering make it a delight. This morning, I saw broods of turkeys picking over snowy cornfields. Hawks circled overhead and, high above them, jets followed the river valley corridor down to Kennedy.

The drive into town normally takes a couple of hours and I was right on schedule as I exited to the Saw Mill Parkway, sped through a scruffy bit of Westchester, and shortly swept onto the Henry Hudson Parkway. One enters the west side of Manhattan Island amid the elegant landscaping of Frederick Law Olmstead, fashioned at the turn-of-the-century to improve the once-muddy river banks where all manner of ferries landed. It is a spectacular route into town, the river on the right, the Palisades standing tall on the west bank.

I exited at 55th, drove over toward St. Patrick's Cathedral, put the car in a lot, then took myself to the Prime Burger for some scrambled eggs and a look at the puzzle. Today is Thursday, the first day of the week when there is any sport in studying whatever obtusities Will Shortz is serving up. Prime Burger waiters are all in those white jackets Pullman porters once wore and I reflected happily on train trips my grandmother and I used to take to visit cousins in Birmingham.

Thusly fortified with breakfast, and the puzzle behind me, I walked the few blocks up Fifth Avenue to America's legendary diamond emporium.

Even though the Christmas rush was past, the crowded first floor at Tiffany & Company promised a brisk day of sales. Eighty percent of Tiffany's business is in gems, and the first floor handles the greater part of those purchases. Of course, the serious stuff, the Schlumberger et al, is upstairs. People buying a $300,000 dinner ring do not want to stand next to a bride and groom slavering over a two-carat rock or a doting auntie from Cincinnati selecting a Peretti key chain to take home to her niece.

The elevators at Tiffany & Company were the last in the city to have operators, beautifully tailored men who sang out the wares at each floor. "Mezzanine: Watch repair, engraving, consultations, fortune telling. Second floor. Crystal, china, porcelain, live rabbits, silver. Flatware, hollowware, vases. Everything, save diapers, for the new baby in your life. The doors are closing. Please step in.' I miss those dapper fellows. A clutch of heavily bundled shoppers and I conducted ourselves to the upper regions of the store. I hopped off at the 6th floor for my appointment with Christopher Burton, a Tiffany archivist.

When Mr. Burton appeared, I immediately sensed we were going to get along beautifully. He was extremely polite, smiled a great deal, and seemed unfazed that I had sparse details on what I was searching for.

He asked if I preferred coffee or tea, sparkling or still water.

After my coffee and two miniature scones arrived, over which we discussed where he was born and where he had studied---Southerners always like to know these things---I began.

"Thank you so much for seeing me, Mr. Burton. As I mentioned in my letter, I am undertaking a bit of research in conjunction with the new Church painting you have doubtless read about. We are having some trouble establishing its provenance. The woman in the portrait is wearing a gold ring. Our town archivist suggested Tiffany would likely have been the manufacturer. She told me Tiffany representatives called on customers at home in the 19th century?"

"Yes, that's quite so," Mr. Burton smiled. "Many of our clients lived fairly close to New York, but because travel in the 1800s was difficult and time-consuming, they weren't able to get into the city as frequently as they liked. Nonetheless, they valued the tradition of Tiffany & Company gifts to mark life's ceremonies---weddings, babies, anniversaries. The obvious solution was to call on them in their homes."

"Do you have records of trips to Hudson, New York?"

"We certainly do. Shortly after the Civil War, we began making regular trips to many of the towns in the Hudson Valley. For many years, the town of Hudson had a number of wealthy, highly discriminating families who were quite good customers of the firm. I understand Hudson is enjoying something of a renaissance these days?"

"Oh, yes! New generations have discovered the town and business is booming once again. You must come up and pay us a visit. If you have any interest in architecture or antiques, you'll positively faint.

"Now, what I need to know about today is a ring. Gold. Monogrammed. The purchase would have been made in the late 1880's or 90's, I would say."

Mr. Burton nodded encouragingly.

"There are a few ways we could look that up. I have a registry of sales made on our road trips. Why don't we begin by reviewing them?"

Mr. Burton disappeared for a few moments and returned wheeling a library cart that held several neatly labeled boxes filled with ledgers.

"In that era, records were all arranged by product within geographic areas. In this way, if someone in the 19th or early 20th century, say, wanted to replace a piece of china or silver flatware, we would be able to source the pattern for reorder. Porcelain is in here, sterling is in this one, no, that's Le Tallec…here we are, jewelry. Here is silver, here is platinum, and…here we are. Gold. You're looking for a ring for a woman? Or a man?"

"I'm not sure. I suppose it could have been for either."

Several minutes passed while he pored over first one book, then another for a later year. He finally looked up at me and smiled.

"Eureka! According to this, Ms. Brooks, in July 1886 we sold a lady's ring to a gentleman in Hudson. Woman's gold signet ring to Mr. F. Church. Size 5. Roman monogram. Two initials. VK."

THE CURATOR BRINGS A LIST TO LUNCH

I drove back to Hudson in a state of high excitement and called Van der Wyck's office.

"William, good afternoon. I need some Church research."

"I am a humble academic at your service, my dear. What are you looking for?"

"I need to know the names of women who worked in the Church household during, say, the last twenty years of his life. Their names, ages, and what they did."

"I will help you in any way I can, but in return, I do wish you would try to convince that *Times* reporter that I am not the Boston Strangler. She drove me to distraction during our interview. I must say, though, she *is* attractive."

Early the next day William called to say he had the list. I invited him to bring it over and join us for lunch. Bennett had made a curry and the house smelled divine.

Waiting for William to arrive, I stood at the dining room window looking west toward the Catskills. The plowed ice in the channel of the river shone like a field of silver quarry stone, but the brightness swiftly faded as gathering clouds shut out the last sun we were likely to see today. I watched the mountains, covered in snow, shade from stark white to sulky gray. The ice in the river, which had gleamed moments before, became sullen and dark.

Beyond the mountains, black clouds had gathered into a wall and the sky toward Albany looked like the bottom of a battleship---cold, dull gray. Trees began to writhe. Powdery snow in the yard kicked up in gusts. The storm moved steadily toward us. Sleet began to ping against the windows. Pea-size pellets quickly covered the porch and little drifts began to form against the railings.

The wind picked up and the black locusts waved their arms wildly in distress. A car's headlights appeared over the crest of the driveway and Van der Wyck emerged, dressed like a Mongol chieftain about to cross the Steppes. The wind whipped at him and sleet covered his coat as he made his way up the path to the back door, clutching his collar with one hand and a vivid crimson wool turban with the other. I let him in, holding tightly to the paned outer door which the wind seemed intent on removing from its hinges.

"Heavens!" exclaimed the curator as he stepped into the mudroom and shook himself like a Labrador retriever. He brushed sleet out of his moustache, pried off both boots and, retrieving a pair of slippers from its pocket, handed his coat and hat to Bennett who carried them away to hang and dry.

"Come in here, my dear, and warm up," I said, steering him into the dining room. William stood before the fire for a few moments, rubbing first his hands, then ears, and finally his corduroy-clad bottom before sinking into a wicker chair piled with pillows.

"On days like this," he sighed, "I try to remember what interested me in the 19th century American Romantic movement. The art of the South Pacific is so terribly intriguing and, God knows, affords a much warmer venue. Why wasn't Gauguin in my future? "

"I think we have a grass skirt somewhere in the costume chest," I answered agreeably.

Bennett reappeared. "May I suggest a little something, Doctor?

Owing to the fineness of the day, I have prepared a pitcher of Bloody Mary's."

"Capital idea, Bennett!" sang Van der Wyck with a broad smile. Bennett returned at once with a tray of drinks and cashews and we settled ourselves around the table, fire roaring and lamps glowing as the wind continued to howl.

"I must say, William," I volunteered, "I'm impressed with the speed of your research--- and grateful."

"Great minds, my dear. I, too, had begun to be obsessed with the woman's identity. Obviously, she is not a member of the family. Convention would have forbidden Church's even glimpsing a female relation's breasts, much less painting them with such obvious affection."

He reached into the pocket of his jacket and extracted several sheets of paper which he unfolded and placed on the dining table, smoothing out the creases. I saw a picture of the full portrait as well as close-ups of several sections.

"These photographs will help to illustrate some key points. Consider the full portrait."

Bennett and I pulled our chairs next to Bill's.

"To our knowledge, and I've been on line or on the phone with six universities, several museums, and the major dealers and galleries---no one can recall any portraits---certainly no nudes---by any artist of the Hudson River School.

"However, as you will recall, the late 19th century saw the emergence of a number of new movements in art. First, we have the American Barbizon. Eilshemus comes to mind. Do you know his work? Here is a picture of a painting he did near the Delaware water gap."

Bennett and I crowded closer. Six nude women floated in a surreal way above a perfectly natural landscape.

"Was Church aware of these new styles of painting emerging in New York and Europe? Of Eakins? Ryder? Of Inness, who began in the Hudson River School, but later migrated to Realism and Impressionism?

When Church traveled to New York in his later life, did he meet with these artists? See new work? We simply don't know.

"Church's greatest works---the meticulously rendered romantic landscapes---were done by the time he was forty. His later works, a few of which we have in the house, were vastly different from his earlier canvasses. They foreshadowed Impressionism."

Van der Wyck sat back and removed his glasses.

"I believe the man's style was changing. Had Church not suffered so terribly with arthritis, rheumatism as it was called then, who knows how his work might have evolved? There is no reason to think a great artist would remain static, forever locked into a particular painterly tradition."

Van der Wyck shuffled the papers and focused our attention to a detail of the background of the portrait. He leaned forward and used a pencil as a pointer. "Look at the brushstrokes here in the background. Clearly looser, freer and more abstract---same subject matter included here as in his earlier works---flora, shards of antiquity---but treated so much differently! This painting has none of the overwrought details of his early work. Sentimentality and Romanticism are absent.

"There's little question the painting was done outdoors, *in situ*. For one thing, he's not going to work on this in a studio where it could be seen by the family. Here and here are traces of pencil sketching, a bit of overpainting here, but not much. He may not have had complete use of his hand and arm but he was still confident of his draftsmanship. My conclusion is that this was done in the last years of his life while he was in Mexico. Not only because of the century plant and other tropical foliage, but because the warm climate would have given his hand and arm the greatest range of movement.

"As I said, our beautiful woman cannot possibly be a member of the family. But! She is a Caucasian, not a local señorita engaged to pose. Another possibility occurred to me---she could be another wealthy---and daring!---Norte Americano wintering in Mexico. But again, convention argues against her posing for him. I agree with what I gather is your train of thought, infinitely more plausible. Perhaps she was a member of the household staff persuaded---and paid---to double as the artist's model? The Churches hired staff from Hudson and neighboring towns and took along some of the household entourage when they traveled.

"After you called, I went through our records. The Churches wintered in Mexico beginning in 1880 until 1899. Here is a list of the women who were with them in those years. What, if anything, this has to do with Sheila's murder, I do not know. That's your department. But I confess the question of woman's identity has been nagging at me."

He handed me the list.

Bennett, who had been scrutinizing the pictures over William's shoulder said, "Perhaps a demi-fluff, doctor? And then I'll serve lunch."

"God bless you, Bennett!" said William. "I'm famished and I fear I'm in for the afternoon!"

The list had only ten names covering eighteen years. Apparently women who worked for the Churches liked them and stayed. The names read:

Maids. Nelly O'Bly, Ellen Fitzhugh, Charlotte Foster, Pearl Young.

Cooks. Adelaide Schoolcraft, Frances Cullen, Sarah Bryan.

Nurses to children. Maureen Shaughnessy, Evelyn Nack, Victoria Keegan.

The children's nurse always traveled with the family during their winter sojourns.

That one name had the initials VK.

It was a place to start.

A VISIT TO THE COURTHOUSE WITH PAUL

Hudson is the seat of Columbia County and as such has an august, neo-classical courthouse.

The brownstone Gothic revival Episcopal Church and the gray granite Roman Catholic Church flank the courthouse on the left, along with rows of well-kept Victorian houses and clapboard apartment houses on either side of the green.

A wooden gazebo stands on the northwest corner of the square, free of any purpose other than ornament. In the 18th or 19th centuries, a gazebo would have been a popular gathering place but the town fathers only got around to putting it up for Hudson's bicentennial in 1984, along with a sign that says 'Keep off gazebo.' Two paths approach the front door of the courthouse diagonally from the corners of the tree-filled lawn past war memorials for WWI, WWII, and Vietnam.

A plywood ramp on one end of the marble stairs makes the courthouse handicapped accessible. A metal detector is arranged just inside. New York State Troopers in severely starched gray gabardine accepted red plastic baskets we filled with our keys, coins, lipstick, and cell phones as we entered.

"I can't see where you are going with this," Paul said as we retrieved our cosmetics, phones, and pocket knives. "We are going to spend a lot of time and inhale a lot of dust and for what? How do we know there is any connection between the woman in the portrait and Sheila's death?"

"Humor me," I said. "Nothing beats primary research."

And so we went into the county archives which contain records dating back to 1785 when the city of Hudson was established.

The court clerk in charge of the archives---an ample redhead wearing a sweatshirt with Sylvester chasing Tweety up a Christmas tree--- was very cooperative.

"What dates did you say you wanted again?" she asked with a smile.

"We need records after the Civil War---starting with the 1880s, please. And we'll go right on up to the turn of the century. We very much appreciate your help," and I gave her a big smile right back.

"I'm going to set you up in here," she said, walking us down a narrow hall and putting us in a long room at a varnished yellow oak table just like the ones in my high school study hall.

"We haven't had any call at all for these in ages, years in most cases, and never in others. What you need is in chronological order on these shelves," and she pointed to six eight foot bookcases filled with ledgers and accordion files.

"It may look like a mess, but you'll find that everything is labeled and in good order so you shouldn't have a problem. It starts up here with 1832 and goes right on up to 1977. The more recent stuff is in another room but the old stuff you're interested in is all in this room. If you run into trouble or have a question, I'll be right around the corner so just come and get me." She smiled again and left us to our work.

"Get out the list," Paul growled, and I put William's list of female household staff from Olana on the table in front of us. We walked over and stared up at the tall shelves filled with files. Paul pulled out 1880 and I selected 1881 as we began looking for those ten names---especially Victoria Keegan---in the town records of Hudson.

Those early years were slow-going at times because the entries had been done in copperplate script. Different clerks had different ways of handling serifs as well as ascenders and descenders but we got the hang of it after awhile.

In the records of the Justice Court, it was interesting to see so many names of families now prominent in the area whose forebears ran afoul of the law for stealing pigs, horses, wire, or sugar. Men who were publicly drunk, forged checks, sold shoddy merchandise, or tried to leave town owing money. Women who were publicly drunk, operated bootleg stills---and ran or worked in houses of prostitution. A lot of the accounts of the infractions were so colorful they could run in this week's .

After three hours, Paul said he'd take us to Cascades for homemade soup and half a sandwich.

"You go and order," I said. "I just want to finish 1897."

The next to the last page listed several arrests made during a raid on a house of ill repute where police had found an underage girl among the prostitutes. Because she was sixteen, she was not charged but was remanded to the Girls' Correction Home, then placed with a local family as staff.

Her name was Victoria Keegan, the name that appeared as one of the Church's nannies.

I hurried down to Cascades to tell Paul.

He said, "That's nice but I'm damned if I see how records for arrests in the 1800's are getting us closer to solving a murder that occurred two weeks ago."

After lunch, we went back.

At four, the clerk came in and said, "We're closing in half an hour. Just wanted to let you know."

The last half hour turned up nothing. We trudged to the Red Dot for a beer and then I drove home watching the sun set behind Mount Merino.

The phone was ringing when I walked in.

There was an inner debate about whether to answer it. I'd had a long day. Helping solve a murder is time-consuming and I had been neglecting work and clients.

After 'hello?' my heart sank. Wrong decision. A new client's voice expressed her concern over how my search for 'original' sleigh beds was going.

The wife shrilled, "You know we need them to be identical. They're for the two twins." I considered saying, 'Better to be redundant than an only child!' but thought better of it.

Bennett walked in while I was on the phone. Like a perfect imitation of Punch, he pantomimed mixing, stirring, and pouring a cocktail and then a question mark. I was so grateful I thought to pantomime a lewd act, gentle reader, but merely smiled wanly and nodded.

Mrs. Syntax continued, "And for myself and Gene, I wanted to make you aware of a change in the Master. I don't see us so much in the Regency like we talked about. I want to go all the way to Empire. I know it's later when he was the emperor but it's still an antique after all.

"Oh, and another thing, honey. I'm dying for a chaise. I saw one in a movie and it's me."

I hardly know where to begin. This woman---who really is the salt of the earth but one where I increase my commissions, remember?--- was introduced to me by Dexter, my roofer, who met the couple at the Red Dot, where the hell else, and got the job reshingling their roof over cocktails (Take that, Mrs. Syntax!) because he is insane enough to work on roofs in winter.

The wife asked him in for coffee one day and said, "You know, I could use some help with this house. All our other houses are in cities and I think I'd like to do something different in the country but I'm at a loss as to where to begin. Ya got enny suggestions, Mr. Roofah?"

So Dexter sent her to me.

As soon as we get this murder solved, I'm going to kill Dexter.

"Mrs. Syntax"---I'm obviously not going to tell you her real name---said I, in my most melodious tones, *"nothing* could be simpler. It makes no difference whatsoever that Regency is English and Empire is French, those countries were bosom buddies back then! The periods combine beautifully. Plus I saw some striking Louis Phillippe tables coming up for auction next week."

"I don't believe I'm familiar with Louie." She sounded worried.

"You'll love him!" I implored. "He knew everybody! I'll come over tomorrow afternoon and bring some pictures."

"Oh, no, honey. Our masoose is coming tomorrow afternoon and then we've got a chamber orchestra thingie after we get her oil off. Let's do it in the morning."

"Tomorrow morning's not good for me, I'm afraid."

"Oh, honey. We have a problem. Dexter told me you weren't difficult like those other decorators," she whimpered.

"Mrs. Syntax, I wouldn't tell this to another soul but I've got an emergency at the courthouse first thing in the morning. Promise me you won't say a word."

"Oh, honey! You in trouble?" She felt my pain.

"Well, let's just say it's a matter of life and death. Not a whisper!"

"You just let us know if you need any help, honey. One phone call from Gene and it rains or doesn't rain, if you know what I mean. And tomorrow afternoon'll be fine. I'll rearrange the masoose."

"You're a darling! I fly to your side! Domani, bella!"

"Ciao, honey," she said.

I hung up and started laughing. I can't tell if my life is going from the sublime to the ridiculous or from the sensible to the insane.

Bennett walked in with my drink on a tray, offered his arm and we strolled into the living room.

"How was our day, Madame?" he inquired.

"Oh, Bennett," I sighed.

The Courthouse Shelves

The next morning, I was waiting at the courthouse for them to open the doors.

As I ran up to her desk, the clerk smiled and said, "Hi, bright eyes. So you're back. Just can't get enough history, eh?"

I said, "Here's some coffee and a cinnamon bun. You were so sweet yesterday, I just wanted to say thanks." My parents taught me to be nice to even the most seemingly insignificant person. Aside from do unto others, you never know who you'll need for a favor, especially in the courthouse.

Back in the long archive room, I stared at the eighty feet of ledgers facing me. Paul had abandoned me and my lost cause, preferring to review Olana's accounting records and attend to other pressing matters---a bungled burglary, a bale of marijuana, and a jilted suitor ramming his girlfriend's mobile home with his truck.

The thought crossed my mind---am I on a totally wild goose chase? Not that it would be the first time. Surrendering to the joy of rote, I settled back into the mechanical process of pulling down the ledgers and slogging through every entry.

After three hours, I found the VK name again in the arrest records twenty-eight years later. Victoria Keegan, arrested for prostitution in 1938, as the Madame of a house, The Happy Man, with her daughter who was 19 and working there as well. Daughter's name listed as Margaret Keegan.

I made a Xerox of the record from yesterday and the one I just found. I grabbed a hot dog for lunch and walked over to see the Hudson city clerk over on Warren Street and look at birth records which they have going back to 1881.

Sitting at a microfiche machine over the course of the afternoon, I learned that in 1882 a daughter, Victoria, was born to Samuel and Helen Keegan.

In 1916, Victoria Keegan had a daughter, Margaret. The place for the father's name was blank.

In 1938, a son was born to Margaret Keegan. His name was listed as John. The place for the father's name was blank.

The next piece of the puzzle could be in any one of three places.

I knew the first place to check was the bureau of record-keeping in Albany where New York name change documentation is kept. Unfortunately, even a request from the sheriff's office wouldn't get a response for some weeks. I faced the same delay if filing a request with the second possibility, the County or Supreme Court where the individual making a name change resides, or finally, in the records of the New York City civil court if you are looking for a renamed urbanite.

Usually only women change their names---when they marry.

I wondered if a man changing his name would be novel enough to stick in a clerk's mind or if the Hudson city clerk of that era was even alive?

I went back to the front desk and caught the clerk just as she was putting on her coat.

"Just one quick question before you go. Who was the city clerk in the Fifties?"

"That would be Mary Queenan. She retired years ago."

"I see. Is Miss Queenan still with us?"

"As far as I know, she is. Lives in Claverack. Still in her house. She's into her nineties now, of course, but a sharp old bird."

THE FORMER CITY CLERK
AND HER FAILED PIE

Mary Queenan's address was in the phone book.

I drove the four miles to Claverack, out past the Plumb-Bronson house and Spook Rock Road. Miss Queenan's house was a little white eyebrow colonial just off the main road. The evening was almost upon us as I knocked on the door. The porch light popped on, the door opened, and I was greeted by a white-haired pixie, with bright blue eyes, in a floral dress, a white cardigan, and a long blue apron. Her hands and most of the apron were covered in flour.

"Yes?" she said.

"I'm sorry to interrupt," I said. "Are you baking a pie?"

"Well, I *am* going to bake a pie, if I can get the darned crust made. The dough has turned on me, I'm afraid."

At that, I let out a whooping laugh. "'Turned on me!' My grandmother used to say that."

"She did? What did she do when that happened?"

"One time I saw her throw the dough on the ceiling."

Now it was Miss Queenan's turn to laugh.

"Who or what are you here for?" she asked.

"I'm here to see you, I believe," I answered, and introduced myself. "Are you the right honorable Mary Queenan?"

"Dear me, right honorable, indeed," she said, smiling.

"Come into my kitchen. Maybe you'll have more luck than I am having."

"I'm doubtful of that, Miss Queenan," I said as we made our way through the immaculate front parlor toward the back of the house. Each piece of furniture was marvelous—Windsor chairs around the dining table, two Queen Anne chests and a sideboard, a lovely small colonial writing desk---and was doubtless passed down through her family. There is something incomparably graceful about the lines of handmade furniture--- and wonderfully reassuring to see fine pieces lovingly maintained by generation after generation.

"My time-honored crust strategy is to keep throwing flour on the dough until it gives up and rolls out," I explained as we reached the kitchen.

I put my coat over the back of a kitchen chair. She handed me the rolling pin and tied the apron around my neck.

"What would you say to a cup of tea?" she asked. "I just now heated the water."

At my 'yes, please,' she took two cups down from hooks beside the window and two saucers from a nearby shelf.

"Want a drop of cold water for that?" she asked leaning around me to inspect the crust's progress.

"No, I have wrestled it into submission now," I answered. I flipped the crust over the rolling pin and slipped it onto the pie pan. She carefully spooned tea leaves into a sterling ball shaped like a small kettle, then lowered it into the teapot.

"Miss Queenan, you have inspired me to attempt scratch pastry again," I remarked as she brought over the tray and we sat down at her kitchen table. "And I thank you for receiving me unannounced." ·

As she poured our tea, she smiled and said, "I suppose you must be here about some ancient court matter, or you wouldn't be addressing me as 'the right honorable'." She passed me my cup and we both took a little sugar and milk, then sipped. "Is that why you are here?"

"Miss Queenan, I'm following my intuition to solve a mystery. I need to know about someone who might have changed his name a long time ago. Women, of course, change their names constantly, every time they marry"---at that she laughed---"but it is so unusual for a *man* to change his name, I wondered if such a thing might have stuck in your memory."

"Was this before or after the War---and don't ask me which war, I'm not as old as I look. How old do you think I look?" she asked, pushing back a strand of hair and touching the pearls at her throat.

I said, "I would peg you at 39 like Jack Benny."

She chuckled. "When are we talking about?"

"This would have been in the early Fifties, maybe 1953 or 1954 as near as I can guess."

"Do you know either of the names? The one he started with or the one he changed it to?"

"The new name is Lucius Wrangel."

She turned her head away to look out the window.

"Why do you want to know?" she asked softly.

"Frankly, I'd rather not say. There is a possibility the man has been involved in a crime. I'm almost certain of it. But I do not know his motive. The name change is only a guess."

"It was a good guess. I certainly do not recall everything that occurred in the almost fifty years I worked in the clerk's office, but, as you say, a man filing for a change of name is quite unusual. I remember this instance mainly because of the name 'Lucius.' I had never heard it before. I asked the young man, who had just graduated high school and was leaving these parts, how he came to choose that name. He said it was a Roman name. He told me he had read it was Roman law that originally made name changes possible. In Rome, when a slave became a free man, naturally he wanted to change his name to put a shackled past behind him. This young man wanted to do the same."

"Do you have any idea why? What were his shackles?" I asked.

"That's quite far in the past now. Don't you think it best to honor the young man's wish to begin anew?"

"Miss Queenan. You are aware a woman was murdered at Olana? I think she had somehow learned some secret about this man. I can call Albany and have them look up the filing. It's only a matter of time. You might as well tell me."

"Do you live here?" she asked.

"Yes. I live several miles out of town."

"You have a slight Southern accent, so I doubt you were born here. When did you come to this area?"

"I've lived here since the late Seventies."

"Do you know anything about our local history?"

"I do."

"Then you know that some decades ago Hudson was a very wicked town. But you have surely heard about those days?"

"Yes."

"So you know about Diamond Street and what went on there?"

"Yes."

"Our young man was born on Diamond Street. His mother worked on Diamond Street, like her mother before her. That is the shame he wanted to escape. He did so not only by leaving town, but by giving himself a new name.

"Most people around here do not read *The New York Times*. However, I do. And, as a consequence, I am aware that the young man who left Hudson and his vulgar past behind so many years ago has more than changed his name, he has *made* a name for himself. I am sorry to hear you feel he has committed a crime, any crime. He felt he had a great deal to protect, I suppose.

"I don't believe I will bake the pie after all. I think I will see you out now and leave you to your work."

Epiphany

The church I attended as a child began its life in a mansion on a hilltop. The ballroom was our nave. Over time, as the parish grew, the vestry and the diocese determined we were ready for a proper building and for two years our congregation put up with construction all around us and then for a few months dispersed entirely to other parishes. We returned to a large cathedral of pale brick.

Our rector had been a physicist with the Manhattan project and entered seminary shortly after the brilliant successes at Hiroshima and Nagasaki. Mr. Russell was famous for giving extremely cerebral sermons during which he would 'go by several perfectly good stopping points' as my parents often remarked driving home after the service.

In the Christian faith, Easter is the pay-off, as it were, celebrating the resurrection and the promise of life-everlasting. But for me, nothing packed the punch of Epiphany.

There is no formal prescription for the Epiphany service and each parish designs its own ceremony. Ours did it up with a bang. David Merrick could not have staged a more satisfying spectacle than our Feast of Lights.

To begin with, we Episcopalians invited the local Greek and Russian Orthodox parishes to celebrate with us, so we had three or four priests wandering around during the ritual instead of just one. Mr. Russell was always bare-headed and wore only a simple white chasuble but the Orthodox prelates' robes and miters were dark brocades shot through with gleaming silver and gold threads. The service began with a festival of Advent hymns and carols followed by the event all thousand of us had all been waiting for, the entrance of the three wise men bearing their gifts.

The great chandeliers gradually dimmed to put the nave into total darkness with only the altar illuminated. Each of us extracted a small candle---stuck through a circle of paper to catch the hot wax---from the hymnal and prayer book racks of our pews. White-robed and gloved acolytes lit their torch candles at the altar, passed the light first to the choir, then moved down the chancel steps to the pews, lighting the candles of those seated on the center aisle. Each person turned and passed the light along to the next person in the pew. Gradually the nave was illuminated entirely by candles. Flickering transitory light. Parents and children all the same, each holding a six inch taper.

We would sing a hymn, usually 'O Come O Come Emmanuel,' in a minor key to lend further mystery and enigma to the goings on. Then a great silence would ensue.

Heralded by terrific blasts from the pipe organ and arrayed in robes worthy of the coronation of Constantine, came the three kings---Caspar, Melchior, and Balthazar. After traveling from Arabia, each king marched slowly up the aisle holding his jeweled coffer high aloft, singing his solo. We all came in on the chorus.

The three kings brought gifts---gold, frankincense, and myrrh. Gold, I knew about, but frankincense and myrrh! Mysterious! And all three gifts tying together the theme of The Big Story. Gold, baby Jesus was a king. Frankincense, incense to worship the son of God. Myrrh, to anoint the body of the dead foreshadowing his destiny. How did they know? As a child, I pondered all these things.

But mainly Epiphany was terrific entertainment. A touch of Peter Pan, the Arabian Nights, and Harry Potter all rolled into one. An exotic cast and glittering costumes and props. The star leading them to the site of a miracle! A treasure hunt! Kings!

The Magi were among my earliest childhood heroes. Three men of great intelligence, education and wealth, they were visited by an angel who told them a star would appear and lead them to their messiah. The story had everything a child wants: Loving devotion, a passionate certainty, and a sense of destiny.

There was even political intrigue! When the wise men got to the general neck of the woods near Bethlehem, they paid a call on Herod, whom every child knows to be an ogre. Herod said, 'When you find the infant, please let me know! I want to meet him, too!' But the wise men were nobody's fools. They did not go back and report to Herod. They went home another way so baby Jesus could finish playing his part in the great story.

Alas, as is so often the case with extravagant beliefs held in tiny minds, my childhood perceptions of Epiphany and the valiant three kings were challenged when I grew up. I met biblical scholars who informed me the trip took so long, by the time the wise men arrived baby Jesus was no longer a baby in a manger, he was practically ready to go to boarding school.

On a Negril holiday, I attended a Feast of Lights in a tiny wooden chapel on the beach. During his homily, the priest informed us the wise men hadn't existed at all, they were a metaphor for all pilgrims. This so contrasted with my memories of the bearded men in fabulous robes bearing significant gifts that I ran out to the sand and wept. The next year, at that same chapel, the priest changed his tune and the wise men were back to being wise men. To do any good, a parable needs to stay a parable.

All of us carry such memories from our early days. As time goes on they recede. It has been many years since I have sat in a nave holding a candle and watching the wise men set gifts before the crèche. Still there is nostalgia.

Tonight being no exception.

The Feast of the Epiphany, to be sure. But we will have no wise men, no carols. Only carefully induced reminiscences and a slim chance of a confession.

The evening of my dinner party, I had set the table with great care and carefully arranged the seating.

The Christmas tree with its lights, garlands, and many years of baubles stood cheerfully in the living room next to the bar. The advent wreath of fir, cedar and eucalyptus studded with holly berries hung above the fireplace. The balcony was swagged with great pine boughs and scarlet bows topped the newel posts.

Huxley came over in the afternoon and was upstairs dressing when Paul arrived.

Only Paul understood what we hoped would ultimately transpire that evening. He brought two officers in street mufti and stationed them upstairs in a darkened guest room where they could hear every word over the balcony. Paul looked handsome in a beautiful charcoal tweed suit. He gave me a kiss hello, rare for him.

"How are you?" he asked, meaning, are you a nervous wreck?

"I'm a little tense but that's to be expected. And sad. Sad that the thing happened at all, of course, and sad about both victims."

"My men are upstairs. We're sticking with the plan we discussed?"

"I think we have to. I think it will work. I don't know that we have much choice."

Huxley came downstairs demanding help with his cufflinks. He greeted Paul by saying, "Dear me! Has the county increased your clothing allowance? You look positively soigné, Sheriff."

Paul replied that Hux should keep a civil tongue in his head or he'd be getting handcuffs instead of cuff links. I left the two men to sort out their cocktails and went into the kitchen to see how Bennett and Michele our helper were faring with the roast.

Another set of headlights popped over the crest of the driveway and stopped. I watched Maureen Lodge and William Van der Wyck walk together into the circle of floodlight and up the path to the door. She had apparently given up on his being the murderer since they tramped along closely arm in arm.

"Darling!" exclaimed Maureen, bursting through the doorway and embracing me through a cloud of Fracas and fifteen feet of cashmere stole, her face flushed and radiant. "How marvelous to be in the country!"

"We've got to get you up here more, Maureen!" exclaimed William, whipping off his coat, helping with her shawl and handing both to Bennett whom Maureen was nuzzling on the cheek.

"Good evening, Professor," Bennett said. "Miss Lodge! You look unusually beautiful this evening! The sounds you hear are Sheriff Whitbeck and Huxley Smythe harassing each other at the bar. Let's take you in as a calming influence."

Two cars arrived simultaneously and I saw Eve and Ted greet each other with what seemed a shy kiss at the foot of the walk. Neither had been here before so I walked down to greet them. I was struck by what an attractive couple they made---but cautioned myself about playing cupid---the man's wife had hardly been dead two weeks. Nonetheless, I remembered what Marks had said about his marriage having died long ago. Que sera, I thought, embracing Eve.

"I'm so glad you're here. Please come in." I turned to give Ted a kiss. "How nice to see you without your attack dogs."

He laughed. "I left them on the porch reading Dickens. They asked when you're coming back."

Once inside, Bennett appeared and said, "Good evening, Miss Eve. I've heard so much about you. And it is very nice to meet you, counselor. Please come in and let's get you a glass of something."

Lucius' car arrived; he had come with his driver. Bennett walked with me down the path to greet them. He arranged for the driver to be ensconced in his cottage and promised food in due course. Lucius wore the blazer with the Romanoff crest and black flannel trousers with evening slippers and a black and gold tie. He threw his arms around me.

"Darling!" he cried. "So good to see you! You mustn't be out here without a coat! Come, let's hurry in!" And we hugged in the foyer as I put away his coat. "This is Twelfth Night," he said. "A holiday I always loved as a child!"

"So did I, Lucius. We're having this dinner party as our Feast of Lights. I hope this evening will be especially memorable for all of us."

The nine of us, drinks in hand, were arrayed around the living room, munching on the smoked salmon Harriet passed. Ted Marks seemed relaxed and chatted amiably with Huxley, Lucius, and Maureen. Eve seemed shy at first so I made a special effort toward introducing her around.

"Maureen, have you met Eve? She's Bill's counterpart on the business side at Church's house."

Maureen exclaimed, "Such a splendid place! I should interview you for my article! Tell me the latest news from Olana!"

"I can report the board has tabled any expansion plans." Eve smiled.

Bennett was brandishing a tray of martinis and after accepting my glass I stood next to Lucius who was regaling Maureen and Huxley with his misadventures during a telephone bidding war two days earlier. I began to hear recountings of other parties, murmurs of intrigues, and odd snatches about global warming and what would happen if the Ross Ice Shelf left its moorings.

Interesting, but not the conversations I needed to make this evening work. Tonight had a purpose. Having been to so many cocktail and dinner parties where the talk devolves into a miasma of verbal wallowing and the numbingly mundane, I often employ conversational gambits, posing questions for guests to promote discourse and stimulate thought. That was my plan for tonight, to set the stage and guide the dialogue toward a necessary conclusion.

Bennett is my accomplice on these occasions. Tonight he began by clinking a bar spoon against his glass and saying, "O Hostess, my Hostess! What question forms in your noble brow?"

I began, "This is January 6th, the feast of the Epiphany, always a special to night to me. On this night in my childhood, I greeted the three kings, and learned that Epiphany is about revelation, discovery, and sharing gifts. And that is what I want for us tonight.

"In a manner of speaking, the wise man who brought us together tonight was Frederic Church, his wonderful house, and the new painting. He was a wise man, but one of many. Before we go into dinner, I would like each of you to present a gift of reminiscence. Share with us the work of another wise man, another artist---and it must be a contemporary of Church!--- whose work has enlightened you."

Maureen asked, "What's wrong with good old charades?"

"Stop it, Maureen," I snapped. "A fortune spent on your education! No wise cracks!

"William, while Maureen is gathering what passes for her wits about her, would you please give us a few remarks about context."

Maureen, happy to be singled out for anything, even censure, giggled like a schoolgirl.

William beamed. "Delighted. Church lived from 1826 to 1900. His lifetime coincided with the emergence of the first American schools of art. Before the 19th century, everything in art belonged to Europe. Church and his contemporaries created schools of art that legitimized America's creativity. The first part of the 19th century---1825 through 1870---was the Romantic Period. This was the period when the Hudson River School flourished and when Church completed his great works, the canvasses that made him famous. There followed the American Renaissance, followed by the beginning of the modern schools---impressionism, cubism and so forth."

Huxley said, "I foresee a great quibbling on dates."

Ted said, "Let me make sure what you're asking. You want us to tell you which artists—Church's contemporaries—meant something to us personally?"

"Exactly!" I said. "Your personal epiphanies inspired by art! Who wants to start?"

Paul stood and gestured to Bennett who refilled his wine glass.

"Lindsey, since I'm undoubtedly the least informed person in this room on art, I'm going to surprise you all by kicking off this little parlor game." Everyone remarked on his bravery.

Paul is a gifted raconteur and his warm voice rang out dramatically as the fire crackled.

"Picture me, a little boy sitting at my grandpa's knee back in the olden days of Hudson. My mother and I were visiting my grandparents and we're all out on the back porch shelling peas. My grandpa tells me he's going to let me in on a little family secret. Naturally, my mom and grandmamma lean in close to hear.

" 'Grandpa!' I said, 'what is it?' He tells me *his* grandmother was an Indian! An Algonquin! Well, I was so excited! But my mother and grandmother were furious and raised Cain, like it was a crime or something. And I guess Indian blood could embarrass some people---but I felt a real pride in it! Indians fascinated me. When we played cowboys and Indians, I was always an Indian. I made teepees in our living room out of quilts. I'd tie a towel around my crotch like a breechcloth and crawl around behind the furniture."

Huxley said, "Oh, I'd pay to see that, wouldn't you, Maureen!"

"When I was in college, I came across the paintings of a man named George Catlin. Catlin was a city boy. He witnessed a delegation of chiefs who'd come east to try to make a land settlement before their people got completely run off by the white settlers. Catlin was mightily impressed with the Indians' dignity in their robes and head dresses. So impressed, in fact, he packed up and followed them back to the Great Plains!

"In the 1830s, he made five trips out west when that was the most dangerous thing in the world to do if you had any fondness for your scalp. For some ten years, he lived with the wildest tribes in the Great Plains--- Comanches, Pawnees, Iowa, Mandans. They treated Catlin with respect--- and he painted what he saw. Their war parties. Buffalo hunts. Their ball games. Portraits of the chiefs. Some of his paintings are primitives because he had to get the images down while they were galloping on horseback. His paintings show us a civilization that has now vanished.

"Catlin admired the Indians. They cherished nature. They worshipped gods. They had rituals and ceremonies. Catlin said they were honest without laws, kept the ten commandments without having heard them preached, and lived without love of money. So, because he enlightened me, and many others, about the true lives of these Native Americans, I'll say George Catlin is a painter whose work brought me an epiphany."

We applauded Paul as he sat down.

Ted stood up and said, "I want to go next. In the same way Paul was fascinated by the Indians and learned about them through the work of George Catlin, as a young man I was fascinated by the Civil War. My granny had a big collection of Civil War memorabilia. I was in her attic one day admiring my great grandfather's uniform and medals. In some old trunks, I found several stacks of *Harpers Illustrated*. That is where I discovered Winslow Homer and the hundreds of illustrations he did throughout the Civil War."

"This was years before he did the seascapes and American pastorals we now associate with Homer," Van der Wyck observed.

Bennett added, "Homer was largely self-taught."

Ted stood in the center of the room and continued.

"Homer was twenty-five when the war began. Harper's initially hired him simply to sketch the photographs Matthew Brady took. But after a few months, the first-hand sketches Homer made right on the battlefield were so impressive, Harper's sent him everywhere throughout the front lines. He'd show a letter from his editor to a commanding officer, Yank or Reb, and then join the ranks and march where the armies went. He recorded the battle of Yorktown, the Army of the Potomac, the Zouaves, the Pennsylvania Cavalry---they actually carried lances into battle! His first-hand sketches of the conflict are among the most powerful and poignant images we have of the Civil War. Life in the trenches. Battlefield surgeries, mail calls, pay days, bivouacs. Sharpshooters and snipers in trees. Women rolling bandages. Parades. All done by Winslow Homer.

"So I'll say his work enlightened me and led me to a deeper understanding---an epiphany, I suppose---about that terrible era in American history."

"I'll say Mary Cassatt," Maureen volunteered. "She was a one-woman epiphany for American art itself because she put us on the map before any of the men. Not only was she America's most important Impressionist---she exhibited in the big 1879 Paris show---she introduced America to France's greatest painters. She came from an affluent family and made her brother Alexander buy a lot of Manet, Monet, Renoir, and Degas. Degas called her their equal.

"That said, it was her subject matter that meant the most to me. Unlike the men who were painting nature, nature, nature and cathedrals, her Impressionism focused on domestic intimacy. Mary Cassatt applied the new painterly techniques to capture scenes of womanhood, of children, and the nursery. She caught the beauty of simple gestures, simple occasions. A woman bathing her child or sharing a breakfast tray. In Cassatt's paintings, the intimate fabric of a mother's life is a thing of beauty. If you examine her work closely, you'll see her observations of mothers and their children on the cusp of the modern era display tremendous sensuality and life force."

Huxley spoke up. "Emboldened by your bravery in revealing a tender side beneath that carapace, Maureen, I will also reveal something."

He paused.

"There is no question my selection will surprise some of you. I choose the man who got Fred Church started in the first place, Thomas Cole, the father of the Hudson River School. However, to satisfy Lindsey's demand that we document our enlightenment, I will specify his series of paintings, 'The Ages of Man.' While I realize some of you may see this as undue sentimentality on the part of the senior member of this little throng, it is not.

"That series of paintings is an important bridge between Blake and the fantasists. It could even be said to be a bridge between the classical and the Christian age. I first saw that work in my freshman year at Dartmouth and I have kept a copy of it on every desk I have had since. It was my introduction to the magic of allegory.

"And, may I observe, lest you think I am unaware of what we oxymoronically refer to as 'popular culture,' the magic of allegory continues to enlighten and presumably inspire---you have only to look at the allegiance of our youth to Star Wars, the Lord of the Rings, even Superman, for God's sake. When everything around us seems to be falling apart, people want something to believe in beyond the commonplace, they want mystery, magic, fairy tales. Even I do."

Lucius said, "Heaven knows I have always found solace in the imaginary."

Huxley replied, "Precisely! We all want a world in which good wins and evil is repudiated and punished."

He looked at me. "Who's the Pollyanna, now, dear!?"

William said, "Huxley, I believe you have allowed us to peer into the depths of your heretofore unglimpsed soul!"

Hux smiled. "Look quickly! The door is closing!"

William said, "I shall offer an equally unexpected choice but one which echoes Huxley's frame of mind. I confess my first great epiphany in art was given me by someone who may surprise you---Howard Pyle."

Bennett, who collects various editions of 'The Water Babies,' cried, "Howard Pyle! A favorite of every child!"

Eve spoke up and said, "But he's an illustrator. Shouldn't you be naming a proper painter, William?"

"He *was* a painter! But instead of being limited to galleries, his work appeared in popular storybooks and magazines! As such, his vast influence on the imagery embedded in the American mind cannot be quantified. He changed the way illustrations look and the way people look at illustrations. Not unlike Cole's 'Ages of Man,' he did a series of illustrations called, 'The Travels of the Souls' which were marvelous. He also gave us the definitive illustrations of Robin Hood and his merry men, King Arthur at Tintagel, Lancelot, the Holy Grail. Every creature alive sees the middle ages through the eyes of Howard Pyle *and* his disciples. His *Book of Pirates* paved the way for Johnny Depp!

"Not only was he a prolific painter, his effect as a *teacher* cannot be overestimated. To begin with, he launched the industry we know as the Wyeth family---first N.C., who gave us Dickens illustrations and Treasure Island, then Andrew, who put Maine on the map, then Jamie who has returned to the costume-based subject matter of his forbears. Pyle also taught Maxfield Parrish, Jessie Smith, Harvey Dunn, Frank Schoonover, and Percy Ivory. He single-handedly launched the Golden Age of illustration in the United States."

Maureen said, "Bennett! Please a drink! I cannot believe my professor has forsaken art in favor of illustration!"

Van der Wyck turned to face Maureen and asked, "Are you suggesting that Pyle's work—or any brilliant illustration, for that matter, is not art?"

"Well, how can it be art if it merely illustrates bedtime stories, fairy tales, and Who's Who in the Old Testament!?"

"How is that different from the biblical, mythical, and historical subject matter of Titian, el Greco, da Vinci, Velasquez, or Michelangelo and Caravaggio, for that matter?"

"Point! Point!" cried Eve, thoroughly enjoying herself and supporting her colleague.

William said, "As an art historian, I would remind you that we must all hope and pray that art reaches the masses! And the masses begin as children! Illustration informs the little minds and awakens their imagination. It enlightens them! Also, and I do believe this from my own childhood, the notions of good and evil are first embodied by these illustrations. When the people on the front page of your paper"---wagging his finger at Maureen-- "have lost their moral compasses, how refreshing to know that we have only to look at Pyle's work to see what bravery or skullduggery look like."

"This evening is taking on a troubling moral tone!" Huxley bellowed. "Have I opened a Pandora's box in which all of you will be confessing the evil side of your natures?!"

Lucius changed the subject. "Has anyone but me noticed we have crept up into the first years of the 20th century?"

"Nothing whatsoever wrong with that," Bennett said firmly. "Church died in 1900 and I thought that made the 20th century fair game, as long as the people started work during Church's lifetime."

"Oh all right!" sighed Huxley. "I knew we were going to quibble over dates. Whom do you insist upon, Lucius?"

Lucius replied, "We have touched on people who were not only popular, but also prolific. There is a much smaller body of work that intrigued me as a young man because of its mystery. The painter pushed

216

the boundaries of art into a mystical realm by flaunting the rules and painting as he wished."

I asked, "And that would be…?"

"Albert Pinkham Ryder. 'Painter of Dreams' as he is called.

"His moody allegorical works draw from all sorts of sources, opera, literature, religion. His canvasses are filled with ominous references or outright images of death. He was a New Englander and even his seascapes have a feeling of terror.

"But beyond the subject matter, Ryder was trying to get at a new way of painting. He wanted to capture a quality of light---or perhaps he fancied he could capture light itself. And he did so through deeply layering color. He piled up the pigment and often didn't allow it to dry before he'd varnish, then varnish again, then paint on top of that. He'd press tobacco juice, wax, anything he could lay his hands on into the glazed wet paint, even used tea bags and ground glass. And it worked! When we read contemporary accounts of his work, all the reviews speak of his achieving a luminosity unlike anything seen before. Both Marsden Hartley and Jackson Pollack idolized him and saw him as the link between tradition and modernism. He created quite a sensation. I have always liked to think that Church visited Ryder at his studio in New York. It is entirely possible—but of course we don't know."

Eve asked, "What became of him?"

Lucius looked toward her, then away. "The painter who wanted to capture light? He went mad. He was unable to escape the demons. We must all find ways to escape. That is perhaps life's greatest epiphany."

I stood and said, "On that note, I'll ask you to come in to dinner."

Michele had lit the fire and the candles. Since we were foregoing an actual church service, I had doubled up on the candles at dinner and we were all bathed in the hospitable gold of the dining room.

Conversation continued as guests circled the table looking for place cards. Paul whispered in my ear as he passed, "God, I hope this works."

Michele helped Bennett serve, then vanished. Bennett closed the doors to the dining room.

I began with a toast. "We are glad to see all of you tonight. And we are grateful to you for your reminiscences. Bennett, will you tell us about our first course."

Bennett smiled. "It's a seared local foie gras over cress drizzled with a hazelnut beurre blanc reduction. It's a little recipe I picked up in the Dordogne."

The foie gras was delicious, as was the eight-hour leg of lamb that followed with its mustard crust and roasted vegetables.

I made a lemon pie of Nigella's and it was extremely well-received. Harriett cleared and we were alone with coffee and the cigars Lucius had brought for the men.

No one wanted cordials but the consensus was that another bottle of Champagne would not be amiss.

Lifting my glass, I said, "Continuing in my vein of sentimentality, the Magi on epiphany brought three gifts. Tonight we gave gifts to each other.

"Gold, the friendship we have around this table.

"Frankincense, for adulation. We lauded several artists whose work has brought meaning to our lives.

"But myrrh. What would be the right analogy for that, a penitential incense for treating the dead in ancient times? We don't actually have myrrh---but I will burn this incense tonight---" and I tossed a briquette of incense into the fire. It began to smolder slowly, releasing a smoky, spicy perfume. "We are burning it in memory of a very beautiful woman who lived many years ago."

"Who might that be?" inquired Lucius.

Huxley had not been briefed on any of this and was clearly a little put off at being out of the loop. He cried, "What? We're having a séance?! Magic at the table?!"

"William," I asked, "Would you bring in our friend?"

"Delighted, my dear." He excused himself and walked out to the butler's pantry.

Paul stood and brought over a folded easel which had been leaning in one corner of the dining room. He opened it and positioned it so everyone had a clear view.

Van der Wyck returned carrying the Church portrait.

He placed it on the easel to the delighted gasps of the guests.

"How marvelous!" everyone cried, except Lucius who sat quietly.

I said, "William has given Bennett and me a wonderful précis on the painting. I wonder if you would share it with us now? Ted, let's have another log on the fire, please."

William began, "This brilliant portrait is unlike any other Church painting. The brush strokes and the handling of the subject matter are far removed from his earlier work and so distinctly forward from the Romantic movement, we can conclude that it was painted in the last years of Church's life while he was in Mexico. Within the suggestion of Mayan ruins and tropical foliage, Church has painted a woman of great loveliness. In his treatment of her face and torso, we see he interprets her beauty as a regal spirit. She is painted as a queen might have been, with respect and delight in her elegance and grace.

"There is a hint of the mysticism of Ryder, the domestic beauty of Cassatt.

"This is not a painting by the Church who was world famous for his depictions of the natural world and its phenomena. This is a Church who in his last days chose a subject who brought him to a higher awareness of individual dignity. We see a reverent intimacy that now gives us a window into this woman's soul.

"Clearly, his subject transported him in time and in technique. This is Church painting as he entered the 20th century."

"My God, William!" exclaimed Huxley. "You're a poet!" William smiled.

"She is so beautiful," Maureen said, "If only we knew who she was."

William continued, "Ah! But we do know!"

Lucius' head turned slowly toward the sound of William's voice but his features were frozen. I glanced at Paul. He watched Lucius but all other eyes were riveted on Van der Wyck or gazed admiringly at the portrait.

"Lindsey has undertaken research about the household staff who accompanied the Churches on their sojourns to Mexico. She has determined that this woman is Victoria Keegan, a young woman from Hudson whom the Churches hired to be their children's nanny. Look closely at the signet ring, it has her monogram, VK. Lindsey learned Church purchased the ring for her from Tiffany & Company."

Maureen turned and put her hand on Lucius' arm playfully.

"So where has the portrait been all these years? Lucius, come clean! Where did you find it!"

"Lucius, we've introduced the woman in the portrait. Isn't this a good time to introduce *you* to everyone, as well?" I asked.

"What does that mean?" he asked. He lifted his eyes to meet mine.

"We both know you weren't born 'Lucius Wrangel'."

After a pause, he said, "How did you determine that?"

I answered, "I suppose the idea crystallized the evening you were reminiscing about your boyhood trips on the Day Liner. Do you recall our conversation on Huxley's porch? You recounted the sights along the river going from north to south, beginning in Hudson and ending in New York City. A child living in New York would have had a voyage of discovery in the opposite direction, upriver from the city. You also remarked on the Livingston's dock at Oak Hill, you remembered the train stations at Barrytown and Rokeby. Lucius, those stations have been gone for decades. Only a local boy would have known those things.

"Lucius, please. Tell us about the portrait."

His voice was emotionless as he began.

"At one point, when she was very young, my grandmother, Victoria Keegan, worked for Church. She had been sent to them as a maid but she got on so well with the children, she became their nanny. In the winters, when the family traveled, she went with them to Mexico.

"In the last years of his life, Church had become very arthritic. His right hand and arm had become virtually useless, he could hardly paint. One day, while they were in Mexico, Church came upon my grandmother wading with his children in a stream. Her blouse and skirt were wet. He helped her step out of the stream and looked at her. She was very beautiful. He asked to paint her. In the afternoons, they would walk to nearby ruins and she posed for him.

"As he painted, they talked. She told him about her past. He tried to persuade her that she could leave that past and step into a future, that she was a person worthy of respect.

"This is what she told my mother, who as you doubtless know, followed her into the family business. Her time with the Church family was the only security, the only respect my grandmother had ever known. When Church died in 1900, she was relieved of her assignments.

"She tried to find other work but failed. Having no other choice, she went back to the old life."

Huxley asked, "What family business are you referring to, Lucius?"

"Whoring, Huxley. My mother and grandmother were prostitutes. They were star attractions on Diamond Street.

"My grandmother kept the portrait in her bedroom in the brothel, as did my mother during her career. You can be certain the only people who ever saw it were not art historians. Most of them probably didn't even know who Church was."

"How did Sheila learn who you were?" I asked softly.

"Her aunt and uncle and I were high school classmates. I had stayed away from Hudson for decades. One of the first times I came back, visiting Olana, Sheila and I went into town for lunch.

"As we were leaving the restaurant, her uncle was walking in. He and I hadn't seen each other in more than fifty years, but I immediately knew who he was. Unfortunately, he also recognized me. I pretended to be baffled by his greeting, of course, when he spoke to me in his usual condescending manner. 'Keegan,' he said. 'Whore's boy! What're you doing behind that beard?'

"I brushed it off. But Sheila, ever the researcher, retrieved her aunt's yearbook. She saw where I had written in it, signed my picture. She matched that to a handwritten note I had sent her after one of our first discussions about my joining the board.

"Slender, I'll grant you, but there it was. I doubt she even bothered to look up any of the official records, but it would have been a very easy thing to do, as you obviously know, Lindsey."

He inclined his head to me and then looked away.

He said bitterly, "None of you can imagine how it felt to be a child living with that shame. None of you has been taunted every day of your lives. It was an agony.

"For as long as I could remember, I wanted to escape. And the moment I came of age, I did so. I worked very hard to make the name I chose for myself stand for something honorable, something respectable. And I succeeded! I have become someone people wanted to know. I am admired. I had succeeded---until I had the misfortune of meeting dear Sheila. Dear, grasping, ambitious Sheila."

Ted Marks face was cold and still.

Lucius turned to him. "Let me enlighten you on two counts. I murdered your wife. And I am sorry. I am sorry that she did not share my values, would not listen to my pleas for her silence. I am sorry she threatened to destroy a life I built very carefully piece by piece."

Van der Wyck, Maureen, and Huxley sat motionless with shock as the story unfolded. I saw Bennett's hand move slowly into his jacket pocket where he had put a derringer as a precaution.

Ted's voice could hardly be heard. "You killed my wife?"

"Yes!" Lucius answered angrily, "but in self-defense! I had no choice! It was a matter of kill or be killed. She intended to destroy me. She had already made my life a living hell, one of Sheila's signature achievements which you know about, I'm sure. She took pleasure in defeating people, first you, then me."

"How did you do it?" Paul asked tersely.

"You mean how did I get the body into the house when it was

teeming with people?

"I had driven up to the house in advance of the van carrying the painting. The drapery to veil the painting and a carpet to lie beneath the easel were in the trunk of my car. Sheila met me in the parking lot. We were alone. She told me she wanted more money to keep her mouth shut. I had already given her several million dollars. She suggested we make a trip to Italy, as if I wanted to spend any more time with her. I demurred. She laughed at me, saying this would be the perfect evening to unveil more than the painting. She always made threats to remind me, always to remind me of who I was and of her advantage.

"The evening sky was such a cold, dark gray. I was wearing gloves. I didn't even think about it. I smiled and said 'The Amalfi coast....perhaps we should, my dear,' then pulled her toward me, as if to embrace her. I pulled her close, and held her, slowly twisting her scarf tighter and tighter around her neck. She only struggled for a moment, then quivered and slumped to her knees. It took scarcely a moment. She hardly made a sound.

"I quickly put the body in the trunk of the car. In a fury, I tore off her clothes. I wanted to humiliate her. I rolled her first in the drapery, then the rug which I secured with a rope. Moments later, the van arrived with the painting. I directed the men to carry the rug in and stand it in the pantry behind the stage.

"I sent the men away, told them I would personally arrange the carpet and drapery. Most of the Olana staff were already downstairs. Van der Wyck met us when we arrived and offered to stay and help me, of course. I told him I needed to be alone with the art for a few last moments. You found my sentiment touching, eh Bill?"

William sat still. His lips parted slightly but he said nothing.

Lucius continued. "You thought I was overcome with sentiment at the last moment. Moved by my own grand gesture, by my insistence no one else see the painting that night until its unveiling. Van der Wyck rounded up any stragglers and I was alone upstairs. It was a fairly simple matter to put the drapery in place, then working behind it, to throw the rope over one of the beams and suspend her."

It was Paul who spoke next.

"We need to go to my office now, Mr. Wrangel."

"Yes, I'm sure we do. May I be spared just a moment to say goodbye to the River? I feel I have only rediscovered it. And now I am sure I won't see it again."

Paul hesitated, then said tersely, "I'll give you one minute."

Wrangel stood, stepped away from the table and walked onto the porch. We all sat silently. Less than a minute passed.

Paul said, "I'm going to get him now."

But Lucius was no longer on the porch.

He had taken the car quietly, leaving his driver in Bennett's cottage. The APB revealed he had driven to a nearby airfield where he got into a small plane. We couldn't find any record of the plane landing anywhere.

At his apartment building, the doorman said Mr. Wrangel had been called away on business. When we went to the GM building, nothing remained of the office except the Jacobean doors and the furniture.

The art was gone, the walls were bare. A note was pinned to his office wall where the Bonnard had hung.

Addressed to me, it said simply:

"When one must disappear, one will. Tell your friend the Sheriff I agree: It doesn't matter where you start.

"What matters is your place at the finish."

EPILOGUE

None of us has seen Lucius since.

I occasionally receive postcards from various remote locales.

A Nice sunset, an atoll in the South Pacific, a Greek island, once a pair of gold earrings from an Istanbul bazaar. I'm sure he is near water, a sea or a coast somewhere.

Paul has used all his resources to track the man, as have I---but Lucius himself is exceedingly resourceful .

We think he left by private plane and hopscotched his way out of this hemisphere. I realize now he had planned for this possibility, stashing money and counterfeited documents in various places around the world. I'm also sure he paid for a different face.

Lucius said he wanted to disappear. My guess is he has done it more thoroughly this time than the last. We have his fingerprints from the party at my house but they aren't in any police or Interpol data base and he is unlikely to kill again. He presented himself to us as a Russian noble. Who knows what new identity he has chosen, what regalia he has adopted as camouflage this time around?

Will we ever catch him? Has he left the Hudson Valley forever this time? There are many other magnificent valleys, of course, many other beautiful places. Still, ours is so special, the quality of light so rare, I keep thinking he'll turn up again.

Not as Lucius, of course. But as a new fugitive from both his old lives. I wonder if he will succeed this time at inventing a new one?

Olana: Beautiful place on high

Church's studio above the fog

Photograph courtesy of Peter Aaron

www.peteraaron.net